Para Salvador,

Please accept a copy of my novel as a sincere homage to your creativity. Delighted to welcome you to New Orleans.

Best wishes

Nicolas Bayer

June 2011

UNA VIDA

A FABLE
OF MUSIC AND THE MIND

by
NICOLAS BAZAN, M.D.

Five Star Publications, Inc.
Chandler, AZ

Linda F. Radke, President
Five Star Publications, Inc.
POB 6698
Chandler, AZ 85246-6698
480-940-8182

www.UnaVidaBook.com

Library of Congress Cataloging-in-Publication Data

Bazan, Nicolas G.
  Una vida: a fable of music and the mind / by Nicolas Bazan.
    p. cm.
ISBN-13: 978-1-58985-112-2
ISBN-10: 1-58985-112-9
  1. Neuroscientists – Fiction. 2. New Orleans (La.) – Fiction. I. Title.
  PS3602.A993V53 2009
  813'.6--dc22

2008030361

EDITOR: Gary Anderson
INTERIOR DESIGN: Koren Publishing Services
COVER DESIGN: Kris Taft Miller
PROJECT MANAGER: Sue DeFabis

Printed in Canada

To all the minds silenced by Alzheimer's.

Prologue

NEW ORLEANS, 2004

The wind crossing Lake Ponchartrain from the north had picked up enough to create whitecaps, which were crashing against the newly restored levee. Two men stopped to inspect the levee's strength and, comforted that it would hold, continued their walk across the campus. The younger man was a robust 55, tall, vaguely Hispanic, and ruggedly built. He wore a loose-fitting light blue linen suit with an ID badge haphazardly clipped to his lapel. It gave his name as Dr. Alvaro Cruz.

His older companion was African-American and exuded an intensity much greater than his height.

A perceptive observer might have noticed that the men kept an exact distance between them, one that was neither familiar nor formal; a unique relationship that had not yet been fully defined and might never be defined.

"Tuesday, too?" the younger man asked, without bothering to conceal his excitement.

"Five days in a row," the older man, Parker, replied with

gratitude in his voice. "She recognized me immediately. Her eyes lit up when I walked into her room."

"I'm giving you the chance to tell the story your way," Cruz said.

Parker nodded and said, "I appreciate that. But right now all I want is to be with her as much as I can."

"For me it was enough to be there at the intersection and know that your paths had crossed again. Maybe that's enough, period."

Cruz's slight accent lifted his words almost to a question.

"No, Dr. Cruz, it's not," Parker replied. "It changed your life as well. Who knows who else it might change?"

Cruz had experienced that power and knew he would be drawing upon it for the rest of his life.

"Then we shall tell it together," he finally said with a nod. "Starting with the dreams that would not leave me alone."

"I verified, by the way," Parker said, "that Charlie Bird never did perform in New Orleans."

The twinkle in Cruz's eyes was unmistakable as he said, "That doesn't mean he didn't perform here privately, now does it?"

Chapter 1

A man with bare feet and wearing a red flower in his vest lapel was playing a banjo in the shadows on the side of a dirt road. A donkey – or was it a mule – galloped by, and a woman was far off...running. He swore he detected a hint of Shalimar. But looking again, the man wasn't there – he couldn't even be sure it had been a man. The sound of the banjo was thrumming from the cornfield. Cruz wondered who the animal belonged to and why the man, who'd looked as though he needed a ride, hadn't mounted it. And what was the woman running from – the man or the mule? The ears of corn, gone brown, were rotting on their stalks – as ravens attacked them. The sky was deep cobalt, clear, and full of currents, like a river. The clouds sped across the sky like stingrays.

Cruz willed time to slow down, at least until he located and identified the banjo player in the cornfield, but time wouldn't slow down; he couldn't get a hold of it, couldn't study it. He was part of an experience larger than himself, and that made Cruz deeply uneasy.

Then he heard a familiar voice – was it Tia Tita? "Follow the dream!"

And Cruz jerked himself awake.

Some people stop to smell the flowers. Alvaro Cruz counted himself one of them. Though he thought himself a man of passions – for food, music, and life in general – he wasn't comfortable around people. From his eighth-floor window at the Neuroscience Center near Charity Hospital, a visitor to Dr. Cruz's office might see a couple hugging each other goodbye or a black mother comforting her squalling baby with a Popsicle already melting in the heat. When Cruz peered down, he saw living brains: walking, talking, running, playing, laughing, sleeping brains. Brains whose living neurons were no use to him yet, because in order to study them they had to be lifted from the living bodies that hosted them.

Cruz saw the serotonin secreted within the brains of the hugging couple, its euphoric effect tempered by the tears of parting. He knew that if the couple were reuniting instead, the effect would be undiluted euphoria, which he could measure precisely if he had the two brains hooked up to his monitors. The human brain, in all its mystery, in all its conditions, from perfect health to disease-ravaged age, was his territory – as familiar to him as his own backyard. Until recently, when the grief had overwhelmed him, he'd been comfortable in that territory.

Gabriel Garcia Marquez once said that "human beings are not born once and for all on the day their mothers give birth to them...Life obliges them over and over again to give birth to themselves." Cruz believed that human brains were built for the urgent program of ongoing re-creation that works like a spark during successful aging. In others, the spark unaccountably failed. In his research, Cruz felt closer than ever before to identifying the triggering keys that failed to work in "unsuccessful aging" of the brain.

But not a day went by during which he wasn't struck by the irony that he was using the very thing he studied to *do* the studying. Even as a child in Tucuman, he'd been relentless in seeking solutions to puzzles.

When he was only six, his father refused to play chess with him anymore, grumbling, "You think too far ahead."

Then, at eight, the course of his life was set when he witnessed his aunt having a grand mal seizure. They were in Salta, on the way to his piano teacher's house, crossing themselves as they passed in front of the Church of La Merced. Cruz could already taste the pistachio ice cream his aunt would buy him after his lesson: mint green with cherries, scooped perfectly from a shiny metal bin, then pressed down into the open end of a flaky sugar cone. Eight-year-old Cruz was passionate about pistachio ice cream. He was imagining the melting ice cream dripping from the cone, making his fingers sticky, when his aunt began to convulse violently, then fell with a thud onto the muddy cobblestone street.

Young Cruz watched in fascinated horror, as though from a great distance that grew greater each moment, as her body flailed like a chicken whose neck had just been wrung. Her feet were shaking as though someone were choking her; she was clawing for her life. Cruz had heard about demons from the priests. An invisible one must be strangling Tia Tita, he decided, despite her having just made the respectful sign of a cross as they passed the church.

He realized later that the coppery taste of fear that flooded into his mouth, a bitter and desperate taste that even the sweetness of ice cream couldn't overpower, was what had triggered the strange distancing impression. He sat in the backseat of the theater watching a movie on the screen that was in a language he didn't understand. In his fascination with what was happening to his aunt and with the way in which he watched it from afar, he would always believe he'd waited a moment too long to cry out for help at the top of his lungs.

The butcher ran out of his shop with bloodied hands. He grabbed hold of Tia Tita and tried to subdue her, getting blood all over her golden dress. It looked as though she were being murdered. People gathered around as the butcher forced a spoon into her mouth "to keep her from swallowing her tongue."

Cruz remembered wondering why anyone would swallow their own tongue. In those days, children learned only as much as their parents thought they needed to know, so Cruz had never been told about his aunt's condition. But there in the sweltering street, he somehow understood that the brain held all the power. It could make things happen that no part of the conscious self could control. In throwing his fastidious Aunt Tita to the street, her brain made it clear that it could exert its own agenda whenever it desired.

That gargantuan, mysterious, arcane entity that had a hand in every aspect of life became the sole focus of Cruz's curiosity from that moment on, the only riddle worthy of his questioning mind. His single, infinitely complex case to crack.

From that day on, the questions of the brain's function, origin, outer limits, and especially ability to turn on the body – its proprietor – haunted, intrigued, bewildered, startled, and inspired Alvaro Cruz. It did all those things, but it also focused him on his own insufficiency, his own impotence – a condition caused by loving his aunt too much. If he had not loved her, he might have cried out in time. The shock of her brain's interference in their love was what had triggered the distancing, he believed.

He had resolved that day to become a detective of the brain and to take absolutely nothing for granted. Not even God who, at that moment, had apparently been looking the other way.

Cruz now stood six feet four and was still built like the rugby player he had been in Argentina, except for the middle section, which had broadened just enough over the years to testify to his abundant taste for gourmet food and wine. A bystander would never guess that he had been a neuroscientist for more than thirty years. His smile was wide, the brown goatee around his mouth and chin not quite heavy enough to obscure the childlike innocence of that eight-year-old boy watching his aunt go down on the cobblestones. His hands were the size of well-worn baseball gloves, soft to touch but rarely missing anything thrown their way. In Spanish, his voice sounded authoritative, but his English voice lifted each sentence with a question, as if he were still studying the etymology of the words. When he was listening deeply he creased his brow to focus, and because he listened often and intently, that crease had grown into a seasoned wrinkle. At the age of fifty-five, Cruz remained as curious as his three-year-old grandson.

Cruz had learned that not only was the brain a worthy adversary, but it was also an immensely complex labyrinth of riddles and crenulations. He was convinced that in the charting of the brain's undulating, ever-changing maze, he would find the key to the overriding secret at the core of it all. He thought of the short poem by Robert Frost: "We dance round in a ring and suppose. / But the Secret sits in the middle, and knows." The "middle" was the synaptic gap. Would unraveling its secrets lead him to the soul, to the spark that elevated inert matter to living being, to the God his wife, Elvira, believed in without question and that Cruz still questioned off and on – whose image and likeness human beings were supposedly fashioned in?

He didn't know. Thinking about Elvira's God only added to the feeling of loss that permeated his being now. What he did know was that the brain was teeming with connections. Nothing linear, nothing inherently unified – just an organ capable of creating an internal reality based upon what the external world showed it. Inarticulate when it came to expressing his sorrow, he was never at a loss for words or excitement when it came to the brain:

"The human brain is a creative organ – it interprets events, not just records them. It functions more like an abstract painter than a realist. Its view of what happens is more important than what actually happened. Pain, smell, taste, touch, and fear are the visionaries of what we see. There is no pure, unmediated seer; no objective reporter. Our images are shaped by the context in which we choose to live. We see what we want to see, hear what we want to hear – or what we need to in order to preserve the image of ourselves and others that provide us with a sense of purpose."

Cruz knew he understood that three-pound oval sphere of connections better than most in his field. But he acknowledged that his lifelong devotion to his vocation was matched in intensity by lifelong frustration – frustration that had been transformed into sorrow with the events of the past few months. Before that, he would come to an exciting find – about the switches that controlled a biochemical pathway of the brain, for example – only to turn the corner and find himself facing another wall. Those pathways were interconnected routes through which one chemical of the brain was converted into another.

A seizure like Aunt Tita's rapidly depleted the brain of energy-providing chemical fuel. Cruz had been fascinated by how that complexity was coordinated so harmoniously, and he'd experimentally tackled the question of how endogenous chemicals might prevent brain demise when adverse conditions arose. Seizures had been a recurring focus of his research, and only a few years ago he'd connected the dots with that early childhood experience. Stroke, age-related macular degeneration, retinitis pigmentosa, epilepsy, Parkinson's and Alzheimer's disease all represent conditions that reflect an intrinsic biochemical signaling failure – like a conductor facing his orchestra after having forgotten the score.

The conundrum that had been occupying Cruz's mind that particular morning was *identity*. How did the ocean of trillions of separate neurons, with billions of points of synaptic connections, hold together a single unified self – a person – with a unique mind of his or her own?

Was the patient with Alzheimer's still "himself?"

Cruz knew he had to reexamine his answer to that question or the sorrow would never go away. Though most neuroscientists made approximations on how the binding of a self was done, in general they relegated such speculation to the bailiwick of the philosopher. In today's neuroscience, specialization was accepted norm and duty. The brain as a whole was simply too vast for any one researcher or one laboratory. Elvira had always told him he was missing the point.

Cruz, trying to never lose sight of the whole, had played the game of specializing in the parts. Much of his research at the Center was focused on trying to understand how essential brain fats contributed to the survival of cells in experimental models of retinal degeneration, stroke, epilepsy, and Alzheimer's. He had simply not completed his mission in time to save his mother.

He thought that the brain may have fundamental signaling to support its organization and that various diseases affected similar events. The failure to counteract such destructive forces gave rise to disease states with loss of brain cells. The keys were in those synaptic portals – they had to be – yet all too many of them remained locked. As the years left to him to solve the riddle continued to dwindle, Cruz had begun to feel an urgency that bordered on desperation. That, he told himself, was why he'd insisted on going to the conference in Rome over Elvira's highly vocal protests.

"Your mother is failing rapidly," she'd said. "She may not be here when you come back."

He cringed to recall his answer: "She isn't here already."

He hadn't meant it the way it sounded. But his wife gave him no opportunity to take back his comment. She'd stormed out of the room – and had barely spoken to him since.

*

The results returned to his desk from the lab in Austin that morning confirmed that he and his team had at last managed to open one more of those mysterious portals. Clinical tests of his new painkiller had demonstrated no apparent adverse effects in thirty-six volunteers; the patent he'd applied for two years ago was now ready for further human application.

After congratulating his research associates, Cruz automatically headed for Elvira's office on the far side of the floor from his own to share the news. Surely she'd want to be among the first to know, despite the wall of silence between them that had continued rising since his mother's funeral. Halfway there, he remembered that she was leaving for Washington that afternoon – and that she'd changed her routine accordingly. She was making her "pro bono" rounds at Malta Park.

Chapter 2

Cruz served on several boards. Some were quite meaningful; others were a part of the obligatory nature of his position at the medical school. One of the more meaningful boards was Malta Park's. Located just off Magazine Street, Malta Park was a private assisted-living facility. The original founders were members of the Order of Malta, a lay Catholic society whose primary mission was to heal the sick and serve the poor. The order was well known for establishing hospitals and other centers for healing in war-torn places around the world. Cruz and Elvira were both members.

Malta Park was an institution that applied the central tenets of the Order of Malta to the everyday needs of the aged. Its St. John's unit had been set aside specifically for patients with Alzheimer's and other dementia-like ailments. There were only twenty-six beds in that unit and they were highly coveted.

As a director, Cruz had headed up committees, contributed to fundraising and awareness, served as the board's research liaison – all of them activities that Elvira saw as convenient excuses to avoid spending time with patients. She, of course, had eagerly volunteered for the "Patient Liaison" committee. When he did see patients and their families, it was usually at some "official business" event, with the staff all smiles because they knew the folks in suits controlled their funding.

"Have you noticed that you're rushing off in twenty-five directions at once?" she would point out to him for the umpteenth time.

"I don't have time for anything else."

"Including real live Alzheimer patients!"

Alvaro bristled.

"I see them every day and late into the night, at the other end of my microscope."

"That's *not* what I meant, and you know it. Sometimes your arrogance astounds me!"

Cruz truly didn't get it at the time. Why was she so angry? She'd told him, when they were courting, that she *loved* his arrogance. From the first years of his career, he'd rationalized that too much exposure to the rawness of human suffering would destroy his effectiveness in the lab. In order to see clearly, he had to focus his vision on his chosen subject: the brain. And though unfortunate, it was a given that the only brain that could be fully explored with the instruments of science was a dead brain. A certain amount of emotional distance was required. Didn't that stand to reason?

Cruz found himself driving on automatic to find Elvira before she left and hoping that she would be interested in his news. To tell the truth, he just hoped she'd speak to him at all. Suddenly he'd felt enormous urgency about the possibility that she might leave New Orleans without communicating with him.

He was greeted by Malta Park's executive director in the

lobby, who said he'd locate "the other Dr. Cruz" and return. Cruz nodded. As he sat down to wait, he felt a resurgence of the hollow feeling that had shadowed his days and darkened his nights since he'd returned, too late, for his mother – in time only for her funeral.

When the director walked in to fetch him, Cruz stood up, relieved.

"She's in 316. I'll take you up."

"You're a busy man," Cruz said. "I'll find my way."

When he got to 316, the door was half open. Like a child, he peeked in to look rather than making himself known right away. Was it cowardice that kept him at the door, he wondered – the fear of facing her; or the need to define the familiar ache at the sight before him? The old man in bed was asleep. Sitting nearby was a man of about fifty, slight in build with gray hair. He wore a flannel shirt and jeans and was sitting on a cushion facing the bed with his eyes half closed. That must be Raymond. He remembered his name from his wife's description. Elvira was sitting in a chair watching.

Cruz stood transfixed at the nearly silent tableaux, still except for the rise and fall of the patient's lungs. The room was calm. All Cruz could hear were the light snores of the man in bed and the white window shade rapping gently from the breeze. He noticed a notebook beside the man in the chair. Cruz checked his watch and realized that he had been standing there for ten minutes. Perhaps he should leave. He didn't understand why Elvira hadn't responded to his presence. Was she ignoring him intentionally? Then he noticed the tear making its way down her cheek. At that moment, Raymond turned his gaze from the bed to Cruz.

"You stood there longer than most," he said without emotion.

"You knew I was here?" Cruz asked, somewhat sheepishly.

"Our senses are amazing things. Who are you visiting?"

Cruz looked down at the yellow-and-black visitor's pass the director had clipped to his shirt pocket.

"My wife."

He nodded to Elvira, who stood stiffly to acknowledge his presence.

"She's told me about you," Raymond said. "You research Alzheimer's, as well."

He wondered how much Elvira had told. Cruz offered his hand.

"Alvaro Cruz…I'm sorry – "

"I was watching you watching us. You looked surprised."

Elvira avoided her husband's eyes.

The two men shook hands.

"I'm Raymond." He invited Cruz in. Cruz smiled gratefully and sat down. "My father."

Raymond nodded at the sleeping man whose gentle snores seemed somehow in synch with the breeze coming through the window; then he plugged in an electric kettle and washed three ceramic cups.

"Tea?" he offered.

Cruz nodded. "I hope I'm not intruding."

Raymond laughed, oblivious to the look exchanged between Cruz and Elvira.

"Intrusion is welcome at this point."

Allowing the feeling of discomfort to wash over him, Cruz assessed this earnest son keeping vigil at his father's bedside.

Then, in his usual blunt way, he asked Raymond, "How do you think he's dealing with it? What do you think is going on in his mind?"

14

Elvira opened her mouth to speak, but then thought better of it.

"That's the good part," Raymond said. "He doesn't have to deal with it – not anymore. I don't believe there really is a *he*. He used to be there, enough to fight back; but he finally gave up, sort of slipped out of himself. I think it's a lot more restful for him to have finally let go of the frustration."

As he spoke, Raymond measured out the tea. The steel in Elvira's eyes turned what might have been elation at hearing his own theory spouted back to an even deeper emptiness.

"How do *you* stand it?" Cruz finally asked over the whistle of the electric kettle.

"My husband's bedside manner isn't his strong point," Elvira said.

Cruz still detected an edge in her voice, but he could also sense that she was starting to soften. Raymond didn't seem at all fazed by the blunt question. He unplugged the kettle and poured the hot water over the loose green tea, which was now sitting in a dark orange-and-brown clay pot.

"You like strong tea?"

"I'm mostly a coffee drinker," Cruz admitted. "Unless it's Argentinean yerba-based *mate*."

"Then you'll like it strong. I know how Dr. Cruz likes hers. We're old friends at this point." Raymond focused on getting the tea just right. He poured three cups, and they sipped the hot green liquid together. "I deal with it an hour at a time," Raymond eventually said. "I like this tea in the morning. It's supposed to rain today." His voice held the exact same timbre each time he spoke.

"Were you praying when I was at the door?" Cruz asked.

"No, just sitting. I come here in the mornings when Dad's asleep and sit with him. Dr. Cruz insisted on sitting quietly with me instead of our usual game of gin rummy, which is the high point of my afternoon routine, when I can find a victim. When I can't, I take refuge at my potter's wheel on the nights when I get – "

"You're a potter?" Cruz interrupted, looking at Elvira, who turned her head to avoid his glance.

"Yeah. Anyway," Raymond went on, "Dad and I used to have this nice comfortable feud going. He was the conservative, emotionless parent who withheld love and I was the hippie kid who left the Navy after Vietnam and joined a commune. We each knew who we were. We had drawn our lines in the sand a long time ago and staked our claims. It was comfortable." Laughing at himself, Raymond turned his gaze to the snoring man. "Not such a monster now, is he? He forgets it all, doesn't remember that we hated each other once. He made his own peace before either of us got the chance to say they were sorry. When he sleeps, I feel at peace with him. I meditate here in the mornings so I can be with him. It's become sort of my temple."

Raymond sipped his tea before going on. "We think we're the conglomerations of all these stories. I never got a chance to see my father as a real person. He always played the villain while I played the role of hero. But now he doesn't remember his role, so why should I? I'm his son, and he's my father. On one hand, my sitting here doesn't do a thing. On the other, it gives me my father. Not as I'd always hoped he'd be, or imagined he was, but just as he is. These morning times remind me that the thing that's most real in us isn't our story or our memories; it's just being here right now. I guess Dad's disease is finally teaching me that."

Raymond raised his cup to his lips and drained it, the gesture somehow reminding Cruz of a priest draining the sacred wine at Mass.

"Life has a harsh way of teaching even the most self-confident of us," Cruz said, realizing he was directing his words as much to his wife as to Raymond.

"You're right. You can't pick your teachers in this world."

Raymond checked his watch and stood up. As Cruz got to his feet quickly to shake Raymond's hand, his left hand knocked his teacup off the table, smashing it. Elvira rushed to clean up the spill. The snoring man's eyes popped open.

"My wife's china!" he shouted. "Didn't I tell you never to come back to my house!"

"We were just leaving," Raymond said calmly.

"Good. Get out!"

As Cruz, Raymond, and Elvira left the room, Raymond's father lay back down, satisfied. It was as if some fit had possessed him, and then evaporated as surely as it had materialized. He was soon fast asleep again. From the door, Cruz watched him, snoring in harmony again with the breeze.

"I'm really sorry about that," Cruz offered. He gave Elvira a hangdog look. "I know I'm the bull in the china shop. Keeping me bent over a microscope might be safer for everyone. Hope I didn't ruin your morning."

Elvira shook her head, and the edge was back. "No, not for everyone. Safer for *you.*"

"Don't worry about it," Raymond said. "I'll just throw another cup tomorrow."

He shook their hands again, and headed for the elevator, leaving the man and his wife to face each other.

"Why did you really come?" Elvira said, allowing Alvaro to take her hand.

Without letting go of it even once, he walked her downstairs and out to the waiting car.

"We got the clearance from Austin. I wanted to tell you the good news in person."

"Oh, thank God. For a minute there, I thought you'd become the Good Samaritan."

They reached the limo and Cruz opened the door for her.

"Is that the way you want to say goodbye to your adoring husband?"

"Is that the reason you came? To tell me about Austin?" She looked him in the eye.

"No, I just didn't want you to – "

Elvira decided she'd heard enough. Placing a finger on his lips, she stood on tiptoes and kissed him.

"Take care of yourself. If you get the opportunity, spend a little time away from the lab. Breaking china isn't the worst thing in the world."

*

The pop of the bottle cap and the clunking of the antique register at the famous old grocery store on Decatur were a welcome relief to Cruz's ears. From that moment, he was officially far away from the digital blips and bleeps that ruled his daily life.

It had been a long week. The good news had buoyed him up, and Elvira, her anger with him showing signs of cooling, was gone for a long weekend helping with the grandson. Cruz felt like a lonely little boy again, with no one to help him hold on to his good mood. Elvira had left him with chicken Marsala in the refrigerator and he normally looked forward to his solitude, but the idea of rattling around in the big empty house was depressing on a day that should be shared with others. Being in a crowd, along with the comfort food, would make him feel better. He would use Elvira's absence to cheat on his diet a little by taking the time to head down to the Quarter. Maybe he could get to Central Grocery before they closed at 5:30.

He parked his car in an outdoor lot on the river side of Decatur near the old Jax Brewery, figuring he'd made it before closing time. But when he walked in, he saw that the lunch-counter stools were already up and the only person around was a teenage boy sweeping the unvarnished wooden floor that sagged from years of foot traffic with no time off for repairs. The bustle of the day was over, and the most famous deli in New Orleans was getting ready to count the money, restock the shelves, and hang it up for the night. Cruz had learned a long time ago not to show up between 11:00 and 2:00 – when the line of aficionados regularly stretched down the block and took up every inch of free space inside the old-fashioned store. Men in suits would sit at the counter side by side with painters, laborers, buggy drivers, and musicians who hadn't eaten since finishing a set in one of the nearby jazz clubs at 3:00 A.M. Down the block they were strangers, but once inside they talked to one another like long-lost drinking buddies about the Saints, the baffling chaos of Louisiana politics, whether the levees would hold in a Level 5 hurricane, or just the simple perfection of the sandwich itself.

The teenager glanced at Cruz, then went back to fetch somebody to the counter. A large Italian man with closely cropped white hair appeared a moment later, still wearing his apron. He moved slowly, clearly worn out from the frenzy of the prolonged lunch rush. The man was typical of the Big Easy, where everything came over-sized: crowds, music, Mardi Gras, hurricanes, catfish, shrimp, strings of speck, sacks of crawfish, and restaurant portions of food and liquor that embodied the word *abbondanza*. Everyone in this town came to expect *lagniappe*, a little extra, as payment for suffering the sour smells and lethargic air that swirled around your head like incense in the cathedral of the profane.

He himself was no exception, Cruz admitted, and a muffaletta from Central was forbidden luxury. But he rarely had time – or took time – for the drive down to the Quarter – and never during lunch hour. Like nearly everyone but the most uninformed, Cruz ignored the generous menu and ordered the muffaletta: cotto salami, ham, mortadella, provolone, and homemade spiced olive salad – a secret concoction that defied even his scientific analysis – sandwiched between fresh, round, soft, sesame seed bread almost as big as a man's face. He could already taste it – sheer perfection. Many a prisoner on Angola's death row had licked the last scrap of olive salad from the corner of his mouth before walking the long walk. Cruz ordered his with a Barq's root beer, the local brand, in a brown long-neck glass bottle. The perfect accompaniment, as the thyme-scented Schroeder Saurus Cabernet 2003 had been the perfect accompaniment for the rib eyes and Argentine chorizo he'd grilled for Elvira and their son Hernan the previous night. Though Nicolas had a family of his own in D.C., the youngest Cruz son still joined his parents for dinner twice a month.

The proprietor made up the sandwich with the care of a surgeon replacing an organ, with loving and ritual precision. All this ramshackle old place had to stand on was the reputation of its sandwiches, and employees never took that fact lightly. Bad word on New Orleans' food traveled fast and could curse a food emporium forever.

As the man handed Cruz the sandwich and opened the root beer with a worn wood-and-metal bottle opener hanging from the counter by a string, Cruz smiled for the first time all day. Gratification was forthcoming and would be instant and complete – a pleasure that, so far, he could only dream of in his work. He grabbed a bag of Zapp's jalapeno chips, thanked the man for the sandwich, and was heading across the street to the river with the root beer in one hand and the brown bag of perfected cholesterol in the other – when singing and the strumming of a banjo captured his attention.

It was October, and despite the Indian summer of the past few days, the air that afternoon seemed almost cool compared to the claustrophobic heat and humidity of September. He could walk the two short blocks without bathing in his own perspiration. Cruz followed the banjo's rhythmic strumming like a mariner inexplicably pulled toward rocks he normally would avoid. He moved toward the sound like a sleepwalker walking across the stage of his own dream.

A voluntary expatriate – whose escape from certain death in Argentina had been due to an almost whimsical serendipity – Cruz hadn't known what to make of their luck, except that it had happened. Elvira never ceased to tell him that unexpected encounters were dancing lessons from the higher consciousness that governs the universe of human life. She had no hesitation in calling that consciousness "God."

But since transplanting his family and his science to this paradoxical Crescent City twenty years earlier, Cruz had felt a stranger to Elvira's God, the God of his Argentinean family. The God who was unable or unwilling to stop the *Guerra Sucia,* the "dirty war" that had killed so many of their countrymen, including Elvira's brother-in-law.

Now, each anomaly Cruz encountered seemed, at first, to be beckoning him toward realignment, to a position where faith and reason could walk hand in hand as equals, but each such encounter proved disappointing. Michelangelo lived in an era when men began to question the interface between the human and the divine: The finger of Adam and the finger of God, as he painted them on the ceiling of the Sistine Chapel in Rome, may have been pointed to each other, but Cruz never failed to notice that the two fingers did not touch. He'd always been attracted to the energy field – static and dynamic at one and the same time – that existed precisely in the gap between the two fingers. He knew the empty space was life's most important locus – the synaptic bridge that allowed communication between one neuron and another, one reality and the next.

An urgent change in pulse rate, as the rhythmic thrumming led him through the maze of stalls in the French Market toward the side that opened to the river, told Cruz he was still hopeful and filled with anticipation, even after all those sometimes frustrating years. And it was the exact feeling he experienced after awakening last night from the recurring lucid dream – the banjo player hidden in a field of corn, and Cruz relentlessly searching through the rows to find the source of the music. Now, however, it was the singing, more than the banjo, that held his attention. The haunting quality of the female voice beckoning him seemed to invoke the genius of the mighty river itself – filled with a life that could turn in an instant from creative to destructive, from the terror of chaos to the calm certitude of hope.

Cruz sat down on a green metal bench meanly curved into a shape that made it impossible to lie down on it for a nap, or a vagrant's night sleep. A wooden plant box, overflowing with exhausted pink geraniums, stood next to the bench and the tall willow growing from the center of the box made Cruz feel even cooler. The edge of the planter was exactly wide enough to make a handy little table for root beer and the half of the sandwich he'd set aside with his chips.

Plenty of others on the River Walk looked only once in the direction of the elderly African-American woman who was singing before continuing on their way. But when a strumming banjo bridged dreams and waking, how could even Cruz not sit down and observe? Doing what he would never normally do – was that breaking china?

The wind shifted and the scents of the market assailed his nostrils – bitter coffee and chicory, beignets frying, pungent okra chopped for gumbo. The babel, with tourists from all over the world bargaining for hot pepper sauce and alligator heads, only underlined the clear purity of the words the woman, reed-like and swaying as though in the wind like a black Orpheus of the afternoon, was intoning:

> The colors of the rainbow
> So bright up in the sky
> Are also on the faces of people passin' by…

The familiar words sorted themselves out in Cruz's memory as he studied the scene on the levee. The mossy smell of the humid afternoon, the earthy pungency of the Mississippi, mist simmering from its muddy surface, framed the moment with significance: the elderly woman alternating song with clarinet; a thin white man in his late fifties, wearing tattered clothing and, over his unnaturally black hair, a trucker's cap with the words "Blues Man" blazoned across the front in permanent magic marker, served as her acolyte, beating time with a wooden foot as he strummed his electric banjo.

Cruz held his breath, as if doing so would keep her singing. This wasn't the man in his dream – this man wore shoes. Cruz settled himself on a nearby bench, careful not to disturb her song as it continued:

> I see friends shakin' hands, sayin', "How do you do?"
> They're really sayin', "I love you."

She held the last note as though it were a kite being wafted on a perfect wind, suspended in the air without effort. He'd listened to Louis Armstrong's "It's a Wonderful World" a thousand times, but had never heard it delivered with the life-and-death poignancy of the old woman on the levee that day.

When she finally let the note fade into the mist, Cruz stood up and walked over to them, placed a twenty-dollar bill in the beat-up clarinet case in front of her.

The man reached to pick it up.

"That money is for her," Cruz said.

"She'll just give it to the next person comes along," the man said. "She crazy in the head. She don't know money. Don't even know her own name. Barely knows she sang a song. I see to it she don't starve herself to death without noticin' that."

Cruz was watching the woman stare at her clarinet as if she were seeing it for the first time. His guilt resurfaced and the sorrow washed over him again as he recognized the familiar emptiness in her eyes that is a manifest symptom of Alzheimer's – he marveled that the insidious disease that crippled the very organ that made us human did not have the power to rob that woman of an art that conjured her last remaining dignity; that not only shined a light on her but also a light on the listener fortunate enough to hear it. He knew all too well that Alzheimer patients often had the physical appearance of anguish, even when they were happy; he imagined, as he had observing his mother's slow but sure deterioration from dinner table to dinner table, that their *angst* was caused by a vestigial awareness of their loss of full consciousness.

The man limped over to her, gently brought the instrument to the woman's lips.

"What's your name?" Cruz asked her.

His question hung in the air, unanswered. The woman had closed her eyes in concentration, then instinctively began to play again, her long wrinkled fingers holding the string of memory that her mind had released.

"Name's Stompleg," the man offered, lifting his wooden clog as though to illustrate, "cuz I tie this here block to the bottom of my foot so's I can play banjo and keep the drum beat at the same time."

Cruz nodded, then gestured toward the woman, whose jazzy clarinet rendition of "When the Saints Go Marching In" now held the rapt attention of the few folks who'd gathered around them on the levee.

"She goes by 'Una Vida,'" Stompleg shrugged. "Guess cuz she brings people to life."

Gooseflesh appeared on Cruz's arms. One perfectly articulated word, one precisely shaped note after another had enchanted the sleepy gathering. For the moment, they ceased being Cajun, or Creole, or Yankee, or Spanish, or French, or Thai, or Russian. They had become one, bonded instantly by music into a collective consciousness that merged with the slow and ceaseless progress of the mighty river. Cruz let his mind slip into their oneness, knowing that somehow he had entered the labyrinth. Maybe if he could penetrate its secret lair, the monstrance of truth – the connection between the physical and the spiritual, the finger of God and the finger of Adam – that had eluded him all those years would finally be his. And the pain would go away.

Chapter 3

It was as if Una Vida's singing created a force field that penetrated to his heart. "One life" was all it took, sometimes, to open a portal that had been walling itself shut.

What surprised Cruz as much as the clarity and power of her last note when she finished the song was the tear he felt running down his cheek. She had touched him to the core, like a mystical escort come to bridge one consciousness with another.

Scientific or not, how could he not linger to speak with her or, if that proved futile, with the gaunt tattooed banjo man – her guardian angel – who'd introduced himself as Stompleg? He would not run away to the isolated sanctity of the lab or of his own office. Cruz stared at Stompleg's black-framed glasses as he listened and learned that the musician was an ex-con, ex-junkie, who'd learned to play blues banjo at one of the top musical schools in the country – where Lead Belly had founded the Prison Blues Curriculum and made it famous – Angola. The grim farm in West Feliciana

Parish boasted more inmates serving life sentences than any other penitentiary in the country. The blues take time to learn, and time was the one thing you could count on at Angola. "The Farm" – 18,000 acres of the richest crop land in the South – was surrounded on three sides by the Mississippi and bordered on the fourth by the Tunica Hills.

"You a doctor?" Stompleg asked. Cruz had absentmindedly left his ID badge clipped to his suit jacket. "I got to thank you, man. I can't tell you how many times Charity Hospital saved my life."

Cruz didn't correct him. A researcher, he had never worked in Charity's ER. Instead he stuck out his big hand to take hold of the one Stompleg had offered. The "Blues Man" clearly wanted to thank somebody, and Cruz didn't see any point in letting details get in his way.

The Spanish name, *Una Vida* – "one life" – struck him immediately. In the Vieux Carre, where everyone thought and talked about the French heritage of New Orleans, Cruz had always been drawn to the older Spanish names. Rue Royale was the name tourists saw on the familiar duplicate street signs, where Cruz's eyes automatically went to the words written beneath it, "Calle Real." Others read "Jackson Square" or "Vieux Carre," but to Cruz it was still Plaza de Armas, as it was from 1763 to 1848, when it was renamed "Jackson Square," in honor of Andrew Jackson, hero of the War of 1812. Although long ago acclimated fully to American culture, at least in its peculiarly foreign manifestation that was New Orleans, Cruz savored his brotherhood with the street signs. He and they, like the Creole *remoulade*, were the solid Spanish foundation beneath the cosmopolitan surface.

"You get a name," Stompleg explained, "and people take to it and start calling you that, and it just becomes your real name. I wouldn't recognize myself if somebody called me by the name my folks give me before knowin' a thing about me. A name given to you at the beginnin' like that – maybe it holds you in place awhile, but it don't tell you who you are, just who someone else wants you to be."

Cruz could see that the woman's name fit the aura that surrounded her, one that he couldn't categorize, a definite exception, a miraculous aberration, and that's what had attracted him to her. All that was alive in her lived in her music.

He stayed to listen for another hour – after all, the house was empty with Elvira gone – and realized that the activity of both singing and playing was a revelation of character more meaningful than any introduction to a person Cruz could remember. The gift offered through her music – melody, rhythm, and a tone almost inhumanly pure and as piercing and uplifting as the Bach trumpets – dispensed with the formal coherent pleasantries that people exchange at first meetings –

I hear friends sayin',
"How do you do?"

– and communicated right to the heart, without pre-amble of acquaintance or familiarity. It was an invitation to explore a wide-open world, one unguarded by a gatekeeper intent on expressing only those things that felt safe.

Suddenly Cruz wished his mother had continued her music. She'd given it up when he moved her from Argentina to New Orleans, refusing even to touch the piano in Cruz's parlor. He remembered her staring at the baby Steinway grand as if it were a disconnected television set. Cruz had the now-jarring image of a living human brain open to him on an examining table. The gatekeeper between him and full understanding was the human skull, and life itself: "Una Vida."

If only Una Vida would speak with him so he could piece

together the life that breathed such notes of unadorned human dignity into the sodden air. As with Odysseus and the Sirens, it was difficult for Cruz to tear himself away from the spell, as mesmerizing as a litany for the dead. Una Vida's aura reached out to him and demanded that he consider it with the full force of his being. Demanded that he give her what he had not given his mother. What if *she* was the woman in his dream?

Stompleg was playing the blues on his banjo, the instrument that Cruz considered one of music's great ironies. Something about its sound forced the listener to feel happy, like watching Cajuns dancing. But using it to play the blues created a unique energy that brought both happiness and tears. The energy was lifting him above the dark clouds. Una Vida sat next to Stompleg, singing words that made no sense in any other language but jazz – the tones and rounded sounds made famous by Satchmo and Ella Fitzgerald came zapping out of her. Cruz closed his eyes to better appreciate the woman's voice, which wove its magic around him and took him away from the world he lived in day by day to a state of *nepenthe,* sheer forgetfulness.

All at once, in the midst of Cruz's reverie, where his body was no longer on a twisted bench next to a wooden planter next to a timeless river but rather had been transported by the river of her song to 1930 when the music she sang was born – everything stopped with a shriek and a pop.

When he opened his eyes, the trance rudely broken, Cruz saw Stompleg's hands moving across his electric banjo and still heard Una Vida's voice, though it was no longer amplified, and the full surround-sound transporting experience of this magical evening had evaporated like the foam on his root beer.

"Dead battery," was all Stompleg said.

He got up, went over to his makeshift amplifier, and disconnected the dead black Sears car battery from the wires leading to the amp. He brought out a new battery from behind his stool and hooked it up. The music was quickly restored. What struck Cruz now, in contrast to the simple aesthetic perfection of the moment before, was the mechanical improvisation that immediately put Stompleg in his good graces. The use of the battery was brilliant, reminding Cruz of a visit he once took to the Amish country with his family when the children were school age. He'd noticed that the Amish carriages used car batteries to power their headlights. So what if the batteries were designed for automobiles and not horse and buggy? The Amish had found an acceptable use of the technology that they otherwise abhorred. Stompleg was far from Amish, but to Cruz it was the same idea – just plain street smarts – and Cruz valued common sense as much as educated genius.

Una Vida's lips had never stopped moving while Stompleg was busy disconnecting the old battery and hooking up the new one. Her neurons continued to fire, regardless of the feedback. Una Vida, oblivious to the external world, was lost in her singing. The sound coming back was incidental – the activity engaging her so deeply internal that stimuli from outside herself served only as a trigger, not as the engine that made her singing go.

Cruz finished his muffaletta and was about to drink his last sip of Barq's and munch his last chip. He'd timed it just right, or else the salt in the olive salad and chips would ignite an unquenchable thirst, which he'd saved the final sip to alleviate. Another great function of the brain. He hadn't been consciously aware of timing it, but his brain's precise inner clock had set him on autopilot, based on its assimilation of previous experience with root beer, chips, and muffalettas.

A tugboat was pushing a freighter across the Mississippi and the people on the River Walk were beginning to thin as tourists made their way to dinner and locals their way home. A mulatta, who'd been watching Cruz interact with Stompleg, gave him a tentative smile as she walked past. A shiver ran up Cruz's spine as he locked eyes with the woman for an instant. Then she was gone.

Cruz decided to put forty dollars in Stompleg's hand and ask him if he would mind *not* playing for a while.

"If you want quiet that bad, Doc, you can go somewheres else, you know," Stompleg joked, pushing the money away.

Cruz insisted, and explained that since he was asking him not to play, he should at least pay for his time.

"Like the government paying farmers not to plant rice," Stompleg laughed. "You're giving me a subsidy, that right?"

"Let's call it payment to let me experiment," Cruz replied enigmatically.

Stompleg scratched his head, then put a "Back in 10 Minutes" sign on his amplifier. He rolled a homemade cigarette, lit it with a Zippo, and blew the first puff of blue smoke toward the Mississippi.

Una Vida continued to sing without accompaniment. Soon enough, the tune changed. After listening for a few minutes, Cruz moved next to her.

"Who's singing that song?" he asked.

Una Vida stopped, as if the wind had asked the question. She didn't respond to anybody in particular, just started speaking.

"Ain't no life. No sir. Ain't no life you want to be living," she said, then resumed singing.

Stompleg had turned and looked at Cruz with a raised eyebrow. Cruz ignored him and focused on Una Vida.

"Somebody's humming a tune; you hear that?" Cruz asked again.

A poem by Zen Master Cho Chu-I popped into his mind:

The reason I don't bother
To strum and pluck?
There's a breeze over the strings
And it plays itself.

Cruz could see that Una Vida's playing and singing was happening as naturally as wind blowing. The resultant melody was as universally pure and true as bird song. The lucidity in Una Vida's voice startled him from his reverie.

"That old song is the 'Jake Liquor Blues,'" she was saying, "made famous by Mr. Ishmon Bracey 'bout 1930. Men used to sing about drinking that old Jake – Jamaican Ginger. We just called it jake. In them days a man drank anything. Some drank Sterno or a slosh of antifreeze, but mos' drank the jake. Make a man so he can't walk right, make him rubber-legged. You couldn't work no more after the jake-leg got you. All you could do was play blues and keep on drinkin', 'cause if'n you stopped you'd take to shakin' worse than afore."

Una Vida finished, slowly rose from the bench, and started making her way down the levee. Cruz followed her.

By 1934, Parker would explain to Cruz later, nearly 100,000 people were affected by jake-leg, unable to work and barely able to walk. Blues songs were written about it – the likes of Tommy Johnson, Daddy Stovepipe, and Mississippi Sarah all recorded tunes about jake.

"Daddy couldn't work the cornfield no more. Couldn't shuck, couldn't have no more children. Plumb weren't no more use for him. Couldn't hardly pay for our little ole clapboard cabin in Iowa with newspapers jammed in the floor and walls to keep us warm in the winter."

Una Vida laughed for a second, then stopped and sat down on the next bench she had come to and exhaled deeply. The memories seemed to be coming of their own accord, as if they, disembodied from her, were trying to account for why she'd been humming the "Jake Liquor Blues." Her crippled brain was striving to reconnect with its functional self.

Somehow, Cruz thought, a whole world of associations had been encoded in that tune, as if the song were a matrix of memory for Una Vida. Her voice was the wind blowing over the strings of the mind, and the music came and went with the wind. It had to be volitional to have the strength to cut through the blockades of disease. If he could discover why music kept this woman's mind vibrant, whole new avenues of research would open before him. It would be the scientific equivalent of parting the Red Sea, and every bit as miraculous. It might redeem him for coming back with too little, too late.

If Cruz hadn't brought the song she was humming to her attention, those memory connections would probably have never been made at that point. He also realized his science rarely made allowances for such communication; being there on the levee to observe her was an anomaly – like broken china. The language of science tended toward the clinical, and the person and the disease became synonymous until the divine spark of humanity could no longer be appreciated. He realized he was experiencing firsthand an encoded language – one encased in a pathway of inaccessible neurological circuits – yet one that beckoned him to see beyond the limitations of the microscope. He would need a bigger lens for this woman, one as big as his own heart and soul as he wanted them to be but knew they were far from being. He wasn't sure he had it in him, though. It was new territory for which he had no map.

Stompleg walked over to them.

"Come on, Una Vida," he said. "This man's clock's about run out and we have a crowd of fresh tourists crossin' over the tracks. They're gonna need some ole Satchmo to help 'em loosen that first greenback from their tight pockets. Time to sing."

Una Vida's body shifted and immediately she seemed fully back in the present, in New Orleans, aware that she had a crowd waiting for her. Then her eyes went blank and she took Stompleg's arm. Cruz followed them. What were Una Vida's choices, and why did she make them? What made her go in and out of consciousness or from one consciousness to another? These were the questions that had raced through Cruz's mind as they resumed their original position at the bench.

He dropped his business card in Una Vida's clarinet case and told Stompleg to get in touch if they needed anything at all. Stompleg nodded, and tipped his "Blues Man" hat.

"I'll be back," Cruz promised.

Elvira was right. It wasn't like him to get involved with people and situations when everything rational in him "knew better." Cruz recognized a new confusion in his mind, one somehow spun off from his haunting dream about a banjo in a cornfield and the way in which sorrow became elation when his wife kissed him goodbye or when he heard Una Vida singing.

After leaving the river, Cruz crossed over to Plaza de Armas. He noticed the mulatta who'd smiled at him on the levee selling pottery in one of the stands in front of the cathedral.

His brain replayed the clarity of Una Vida's singing, and the elation washed over him again.

*

A horse – no, looked like a mule – bearing a rider stopped at the side of a dirt road. When the rider dismounted – more like fell off – he could see she was a woman. Within the dream,

Cruz closed his eyes to make the vision clear. *She ran into the cornfield, lured by the sound of a banjo. The sky was deep cobalt that shimmered in the heat, full of currents, more like river than air. The clouds fled toward the horizon like stingrays. The corn plants had gone brown. The wind rattled the rotting stalks. The rattle seemed to speak the words again, "Follow the dream." The words were repeated, this time in a voice he recognized clearly – as his mother's.*

Again Cruz willed it all to slow down, long enough for him to find the man playing the banjo. Somehow, he knew the woman had brought the mule to take the man away, but he also knew somehow that the man kept playing because he couldn't get on the mule. He was lost in the corn; couldn't even see the mule. The fetid air of the dying field filled Cruz's nostrils. The clouds wouldn't slow down and the music played faster. He couldn't find the man; couldn't study the situation. He was failing a test he didn't understand, part of the play but not its director. And that made him uneasy.

He jolted awake, trying to recapture the lucid dream with his conscious mind before its crucial details eluded him forever.

Driving home the night before, the encounter with Una Vida had haunted Cruz in a way that felt very similar to the mesmerizing impact of his recurring dream, which had revisited him even more strongly. His mother's voice in the dream – had she forgiven him for not being there for her? Did she even know he wasn't? It hammered him over the head to pay attention. He played every detail of the encounter, like the dream, over and over again in his mind like a favorite movie, looking for anything he might have missed about the events of that afternoon and evening.

There had to be something.

Chapter 4

On their drive home Sunday evening, in much less detail than usual, Elvira reported to her husband how things were going with Nicolas and their new grandson. When she fell silent, Cruz related the entire story of Una Vida, including the uncanny connection between his banjo dreams and Stompleg's instrument that had drawn him to the levee.

He'd driven to Louis Armstrong International with virtually zero awareness of the drive and was startled to realize he was approaching the Passenger Pickup curb. The images evoked by his strange encounter near the river had followed one another and occupied his mind. It was part of the mystery of the brain that made him sometimes think consciousness was vastly overrated: Before we know it, we were in the car on the way to somewhere familiar – home, or work, or airport – and got there somehow without knowing how we did it. He remembered one day arriving home and pulling into the drive, realizing he couldn't recall if he'd taken Claiborne Avenue or St. Charles.

Consciousness wasn't a continuous experience, then; it ebbed and flowed. We generally thought of the two main states as asleep and awake, but they were only the beginning. At any moment throughout the day our brains were functioning at varying levels of attunement and engagement. While playing a competitive game of tennis, one of Cruz's favorite sports, his brain would be fully engaged in a few quickly alternating tasks: watch the ball, run, hit, jump, get ready, watch the ball, slam, volley. There wasn't much room for thinking about the state of affairs in the Middle East or about what he would eat for dinner, though the brain could certainly handle all that; but when it tried, the usual result was blowing the shot. Cruz knew that was a simplification; our states of awareness were as varied as the shapes of snowflakes. They were completely unique, came one after another in a flurry, and by the time we stopped to study them had already melted away.

"What do you think?" he asked his wife.

The stability of Elvira's presence in his life was like a touchstone to him. He couldn't exist without her. Her not being in his life was unthinkable. He hated it when she was unhappy with him. Reality wasn't real, didn't become part of their history, until he'd reported it to her and she had commented upon it.

"I think it's a good thing that you're interested in Una Vida," she said.

He could almost see her biting her tongue, keeping herself from saying, "It's just too bad you weren't interested in your own mother enough to be at her deathbed."

The feeling of relief was tangible when, instead, she leaned across to kiss him, on the cheek this time – to let him know that all was forgiven, her usual signal that the fight was over.

"I have to admit I missed you," she chuckled.

Cruz returned her laugh and squeezed her hand. Having her back put it all into perspective.

"Where shall I go from here?" he asked. "Forget it?"

To the casual observer, Elvira's slender build, gentle demeanor, and steady voice might allow her to be mistaken for someone who was passive. Elvira was anything but. To underestimate her was like the rock in a stream underestimating the power of the water rushing over it daily.

"You obviously shouldn't forget it," she smiled. "And you've already done what you needed to do for now."

"What do you mean?"

"You left your business card. Now let's see what fate wants to do with you.

*

The rest of the evening was given over to the rituals of a loving homecoming and Cruz's mind focused on sensation and celebration.

As a result, he felt more rested and relaxed than usual when he arrived at the Center to face his over-sized desk and noted the accumulation from the day before. Some days he wished the stacks of paperwork piled like foothills on the antique oak surface would be washed away overnight by a supernatural hand. Instead, his assistant, Zevie, had placed them neatly into stacks that organized and properly collated the results of experiments performed on the floors above and beneath him. Zevie had been his executive assistant for sixteen years and knew her boss the way a great *sous-chef* knows her master chef – she always had all the ingredients at hand at precisely the right time and made the Center come together because of her relentless attention to detail. She was not there to judge, only to assist.

He continued to imagine the washing away of paper as he made his selective rounds, like Mary Poppins inspecting the children's nursery and teaching them to snap their fingers so the toys would put themselves away. He chose a different lab to stop in randomly each day.

The visitation concluded, Cruz approached the mountain of results, his climbing tools provided by Zevie, and went about the day's business of scaling it. It was nine by the time he returned to his office, where he usually worked uninterrupted until 10:30. By that time he was normally called to an experiment being performed or to attend to a rehearsal of a seminar or Ph.D. thesis defense. He imagined the large hallways of the Center as a crowded freeway of neuronal activity. To keep the place – an enormous brain all its own – functioning well, everyone had to be in constant movement ferrying information back and forth.

The movement was both ordered and improvised, and Cruz liked to think of himself as the unlikely conductor of a jazz band. He loved the order but insisted on the improvisation because, like any successful scientist, he knew that discoveries were often made by serendipity resulting from unexpected juxtapositions. And he'd always noticed that quantity and quality were causally connected; it had taken Edison thousands of attempts to find the right filament for his light bulb. Cruz opened the Center to the widest variety of research – from studies of the inner ear of Louisiana terrapins (because they most closely resembled the human ear) to autopsies of recently deceased brains that had been rushed from Charity Hospital's Emergency Room (because the deterioration of our controlling organ is rapid, post mortem). Despite the five projects he himself was working on, all carefully being moved to the next step like players on an invisible chess board, he listened to his team with the ear of a Duke Ellington, totally in tune with his players.

In his research over the last few years, Cruz and his collaborators had discovered the process by which certain neurons could actually rescue themselves after injury and prevent death. His self-imposed mission was to translate the concrete reality he saw under the microscope (or had imaged by molecular exploration) to the continuous progress of mankind toward total self-awareness.

One of the things about the human brain that always kept Cruz in awe was that it was not a closed system set in stone. Its very structure was built to create new concepts, to reshape reality, and to promote progress through imagination. Electricity – a computer – has specific wires, circuit-pathways across which messages of intention pass. But the brain possesses choice at every step. One neuron can't talk to another without crossing the empty gap of a synapse. This was where communication happens, and it's a lock-and-key event. There's no continuity between the end of one neuron and the beginning of another; there's always that gap in which a choice must be made.

The act of free will could never be fully programmed; for Cruz, that endless series of choices was nothing short of a miracle of nature. He would argue to Elvira that his personal contact with the spiritual dimension of life was that every waking minute in the life of the brain he studied was mysterious.

When his colleagues at Harvard and MIT hooked up electrodes to Tibetan and Zen masters to measure what happened in their brains during meditation, Cruz paid attention. What fascinated him was their experience of no-self. In certain kinds of passive meditation practices, parts of the brain that perceived a separate self apparently were blocked, thereby achieving the state referred to as "transcendence." Was that what his mother experienced when she capitulated to the disease that finally took her life?

Usually, the brain has a sort of internal GPS system that signals to us exactly where we are in relation to any object we're viewing. If we stand in the middle of a garden watching a bee gather nectar from a pink rose, our brains will not only note the shape and position of the bee and the rose, but also exactly where we are in relation to that picture. But according to the experience of highly disciplined and experienced meditators, that internal GPS system can be temporarily turned off. All the brain perceives then is the rose and the bee. The viewer can simply have the experience of being the rose or the bee interchangeably – and that's all: no self-referencing. The meditator experiences pure absorption, becoming one with the object in view and not being separated by the brain's constructed barrier of self. It's said that the experience is accompanied by great peace and calm. He had seen that calm on Una Vida's face.

Cruz longed to feel it himself but knew it wouldn't come to him through meditation or through anything associated with religion or prayer. He was set on finding it within his chosen realm, that of science; and had always believed that persistence would take him there. From time to time he'd tried to explain all this to others.

"You're too intense," he often heard.

The only exception was his wife. Elvira at least partly understood him.

"You always take the hardest road," she would tease. "It's your macho nature."

"I'm a physician-scientist," he would argue. "I don't want to confuse myself with anything that could take away my focus on the molecular mechanisms of the mind and on how brain cells survive when confronted by adversity."

"You're a doctor," Elvira would reply, "or you're an ass. No doctor is an island," or the familiar, "Brains work best in people," but her attacks had always been playful until the past few months.

Dante Alighieri wrote that in order to understand the

whole, one must understand every part, and that every part reflected the whole. Oblivious to the gentle ribbing of others, Cruz consoled himself with Dante's double-edged observation, committed to continuing his study of the parts in order to master the whole. What was the precise harmonic of the brain's electrochemical pulses? Was there, in the harmony and rhythms of the well-tempered mind, a discernible aesthetic? Would we ever clearly be able to define the music of the sphere known as the brain? Was the brain one with the mind, and how were mind and heart connected? Meanwhile, he'd continued to remind his colleagues at the lab that they must focus their primary energy on data and quantifiable results from well designed and well performed experiments.

When Cruz found a moment to breathe, he walked to the window to look out on the city where jazz was born and thought how experimentation was both the inside and outside atmosphere of the life he and Elvira had created there.

*

Cruz was reviewing the most recent data when the strum of a banjo entered his head unbidden. It occurred to him that the man in his dream couldn't get on that mule because he couldn't stay on; his legs were too wobbly or bowed. Was he Una Vida's father? Was it the jake-leg that kept the man in the corn?

The song in the dream, he suddenly remembered, was "When the Saints Come Marchin' In." Wasn't it Jesus who would come back to Jerusalem on a mule – or was that a donkey? And why was he smelling Shalimar in the dream? Image after image and association after association flooded into Cruz's mind as he lifted his eyes off the data arranged in neat, orderly rows on the spreadsheets. A daydreaming or wandering mind wasn't a miracle; a focused one was. With

43

so many realms to explore, the brain had to wear blinders to the vast majority of them to solve even a simple math problem. Keeping his mind focused had never been difficult for Cruz before – but it was now.

At one o'clock Zevie poked her head in to let Cruz know that he was awaited in the conference room. Three officials from a federal funding agency, including his old friend, Morton Friedman, were waiting with laptops and Blackberries, ready to grill him on the results of sleep deprivation – for purposes he was afraid to imagine. But Friedman's agency was a major funding source for the Center, so he greeted them with a smile.

Cruz got through the meeting with a near-guarantee that the review would support funding for the next three years. The officials, especially Morton, were impressed with the early results and with the precision of the methodology. Cruz spoke about "performance degradation" and about the next steps of his research, explaining to them that one of his greatest concerns was that the importance of dreaming in humans wasn't fully understood. What would happen if a person couldn't dream for five nights straight? In the unbelievable system that was the human brain, Cruz found it difficult to believe that dreaming was just *lagniappe* – that extra something we could do just as well without. Like other brain operations, the dream process had to be essential to optimal brain function.

What he didn't mention to Morton Friedman was his nagging sense that dreams might function as avenues by which humans could depart from the realm of consciously measurable reality and access realms referred to as "parapsychological," "paranormal," "supernatural," "otherworldly," "imaginary," "fantastic," "artistic." No, it was probably wise that he hadn't gone there with the feds.

Morton and his colleagues pumped Dr. Cruz's hand

with congratulations and closed up their devices to leave for the airport. The red-haired woman lingered a minute, the last to close her laptop and return it to a black case identical to those of her associates.

"Some things we don't have to say," she winked at him conspiratorially, as though she'd read his mind. She removed her dark round-frame glasses and looked right at Cruz. "Data is one thing, dreams are another." The woman spoke flatly, replaced the glasses on her face, then walked out the door double-time to catch up with the others.

Cruz, letting her comment slide, followed the woman out to formally see the group off at the elevator. On his way through the lobby, Zevie passed him a note, but in her deft way so the officials didn't see the exchange.

The note read: "Crying woman called. Says she knows Una Vida. Must talk to you. Waiting in St. Anthony's Garden. Are you OK?"

It had been their tradition to never discuss the content of a note, which Zevie always wrote in telegram style, and rarely did she end one with a question of her own.

Cruz told her he would take lunch out of the Center, and though she didn't lift her head from her screen, he could see a spike of worry moving up her spine. A lunch out of the lab hardly ever happened unless there was a conference in town or an important research working lunch. Friday's excursion had been a definite aberration and a Monday outside lunch was unheard of, but Zevie knew him too well, and telling her that he was suddenly following the pull of intuition would only worry her more. Making his recent behavior doubly baffling was the fact that he was going to lose precious lab time the following week while meeting with colleagues in Madrid.

Cruz left the lab but didn't feel like getting into his car, driving to the Quarter, and dealing with the hassle of parking there. It was cool enough, so he decided to walk to the streetcar stop on Canal Street. As he waited to board, he looked above him at the sumptuous blue sky. Its quickly moving clouds brought him back to the dream – or was the dream bringing him to this sky?

Cruz boarded the streetcar, leaned out the open window, and breathed in the dreaming sky. The clouds didn't need rails to run on. They flew freely, without impediment, moved on ahead of the streetcar, and never looked back.

*

He got off the train, which was nearly empty of anyone but locals despite it being high season, in front of Harrah's Casino. The walk up Decatur Street to Plaza de Armas took only a few minutes and it felt good to stretch his legs after the conference room meeting. He listened for the strains of a banjo as he approached the plaza, but the breeze was blowing toward the river and the sound eluded him.

The usual tourist buggies were lined up along the wrought iron fence that surrounded the plaza.

He couldn't help himself and asked one of the drivers, "Are these mules or donkeys?"

"Mules," the gravelly-voiced man with the black hat answered, as though that exact question was to be expected from a man wearing a suit.

Cruz noticed that both the driver and his mule wore a red carnation. The man doffed his hat respectfully.

"Take a ride. Ole Handsome John will show you what the Big Easy's all about. Been drivin' this buggy goin' on fifty years – ain't a thing happen in this town I don't know 'bout."

"I'll take a rain check," Cruz smiled.

A man driving a mule might well be in his future. Ignoring the driver's look, he walked through the gates into the plaza, making his way past the artists selling oils or water-colors of the city and bayous – and offering to do a portrait of him on the spot. But the surroundings were familiar.

It took a few minutes after the harsh light in the plaza for his eyes to adjust to the stained glass-lit dimness inside the cathedral. In 1987, Pope John Paul II had paid a visit to St. Louis Cathedral, the oldest in the state, and had blessed three million of the faithful. Cruz and Elvira had been among them, at her insistence, and they thanked God for their good fortune in having found a new home in that vibrant and hospitable city.

One by one, familiar images of death, resurrection, punishment, and salvation came into focus. He knelt down, paid his respects, then stood and made his way to the back door of the cathedral, where the blue sky greeted him again as if it had simply been playing a game of hide and seek.

He'd never been to the cathedral garden. As soon as he saw the statue of St. Anthony, a strange feeling of affinity for the emaciated saint overcame him. The statue depicted the saint at the height of his physical prowess, arms raised high in triumph as if he'd just thrown off the last demon that had been trying to tempt him.

The life of St. Anthony was one of the most austere stories he'd ever heard. Born in the middle of the third century, in Greece, the ascetic lived to well over 100. Both his parents died when he was twenty and left him a rich man. Nonetheless, he felt lost, empty, and convinced that material possessions were more of a burden than a comfort, so he gave them all away to follow the teachings of Christ and took up residence in a tomb, living as a hermit for fifteen years. When he emerged from the tomb for a brief time at the age of thirty-five to teach, his face had grown gaunt to the point that his cheekbones had become his most pronounced feature – except for his eyes, which people called "the fire that could warm anyone who dared looking into them."

Given his own passion, his pursuit of the vocation of the brain, Cruz admired intensity. He admired the saint's dedication to a spirit not of this world and found himself somewhat jealous of it. Cruz strived for that kind of conviction, believing it was immoral not to live every second of your life with the utmost intensity.

The woman who had phoned him for this strange rendezvous behind the cathedral was now standing nearby.

"I am Alvaro Cruz," he said, offering his hand as he approached. "Did you call my office?"

The woman, a striking mulatta, looked to be in her late thirties, tall and quite slender; she was wearing a long, flowing cotton skirt of an indeterminate bluish-green. He recognized her as the woman who'd smiled at him on the levee. She appeared stylistically lost in time, an impression confirmed by her brown leather sandals – the kind that last forever – with flat leather soles and worn toes. Her skin, the color of latte, looked comfortable and well-worn, with a complexion that came from spending much of her life outdoors. Cruz found it hard to imagine her in an office or lab.

The woman was watching a ladybug that was crawling across her left big toe. At the sound of Cruz's voice, she raised her head quickly and her long dark-brown straight hair, highlighted with gray, fell back to reveal a face completely unadorned by makeup, unmarred by any hint of affectation. Her eyes were the violet color you see right after sunset and before the full weight of darkness chases away the vestiges of day. Her eyes made him soften his tone as he repeated his question.

"Do you believe all of this?" she asked, nodding at the statue and gesturing toward the church.

"I am a Catholic, if that's what you mean."

"A lapsed Catholic or a practicing Catholic?"

"Practicing," he answered. "More or less."

"My grandmother was religious; so was my mother," the woman said after pausing to weigh his answer.

"What can I do for you?" he asked.

From a tiny burlap purse, she pulled out a piece of pink paper with purple writing on it. The letters were in calligraphy and recorded all of Cruz's information: phone numbers, email, titles, and address. He'd never seen such information, much less his own, presented as a deliberate art form.

"Do you make a habit of leaving your contact information with street musicians?"

"Is that where you got it?"

"I certainly didn't get it off the Internet," she said. "Do you have any idea who that old woman is down by the river? Are you really interested in her?"

"I don't know who she is," Cruz said, "but I'd like to find out."

"You're a scientist. You want to study her?"

"In a manner of speaking," Cruz said, instinctively holding back.

"She's not able to consent to anything, let alone consent to being your science experiment."

Cruz watched the anger flash across her face, then witnessed the turmoil of emotions beneath the surface and recognized the handiwork of fear. She looked as if she were about to bolt.

"Nothing so invasive as that. I'm just very curious about her."

"You're just amusing yourself, is that it? Forget it! Why would I even think – "

She stopped mid-sentence, grabbed up her things, then offered Cruz the pink paper. He made no move to take it, so she dropped it at his feet. As she walked away, the paper swirled to the ground like a whirligig.

"So that's it?" he called after her. "You phone my office. I leave my lab in the middle of a busy Monday and come down here to have you tell me I'm amusing myself? If I didn't care, why do you think I came to meet you?"

She turned momentarily to look into Cruz's eyes. Then she started quickly through the side gate into Pirate's Alley.

"How do you know Una Vida?" he called after her, ignoring the people who were stopping to stare, but the woman had disappeared already, darting into the crowd like a frightened rabbit, and Cruz found himself heading after her.

She turned toward Faulkner House, his favorite bookstore, and was heading toward the plaza. Cruz followed, barely able to keep her in sight in the crush of early revelers heading for Bourbon Street. By the time the buggy crossed his path, he'd lost sight of her. Cruz returned to the cathedral garden and retrieved the piece of pink paper, folded it, and tucked it inside his suit jacket.

"Guess I said the wrong thing," he murmured.

*

Without consciously intending it, Cruz found himself back on the river levee where he'd first encountered Una Vida. He sat on the same bench beside the wooden planter with its graceful willow. Despite the heedless southerly progress of the river, the place seemed empty of life, like a theater after the performance.

Alzheimer's, Cruz reflected, was the disease that closed the theater – the director had abandoned the play and the actors and audience no longer knew what to do. It was the disease that caused parents to not remember the names of their children, the name of the hotel where they'd honeymooned, or the first taste of chocolate they'd been given by a favorite aunt. They couldn't remember the feeling of lying down in freshly fallen white snow and extending their arms and legs to make an angel. But Elvira believed Alzheimer's victims could *feel* many things – things they were no longer able to consciously express. Una Vida was living proof of his wife's hypothesis; that had to explain his compulsion to get to the bottom of her story.

Music is one of those central universal human experiences that never go away. Its immediacy and its pulsing life require presence in the present, not memory of the past. That was what intrigued Cruz the most about Una Vida. What did music have to teach him about the nature of the disease he worked so many hours a day trying to unravel? Perhaps more importantly, what did music have to teach him about human dignity and its continued expression despite the loss of the ability to remember how to feed oneself or even relieve oneself? Her brain once had been a vast universe that was now slipping into its original undifferentiated immediacy and was progressively – irreversibly – losing its ability to describe its reality to others. Yet in her music, Una Vida's brain was somehow still able to embody a life that included others and welcomed them to explore something universally true to human experience.

He carefully reviewed the situation. The first step was always case history. Without sufficient data, no theory could be formulated. For that, he needed to know Una Vida's real name. With or without the mystery woman and Stompleg, he would find a way. Outside the lab. Elvira would be proud.

As he gazed in reverie at the spot Una Vida and Stompleg had occupied, Cruz felt an inexplicable sense of emptiness and loss overwhelm him again. He took the pink paper from his pocket and wondered what the calligraphy could tell him. Clearly, the new stranger was herself an artist. Maybe he could ask around, canvas the street artists that lined Plaza de Armas.

Cruz scolded himself. He'd said the wrong thing and missed an opportunity. He'd failed his audition. He wouldn't fail again. He'd enlist what he'd long ago identified as the most important tool in his prodigious arsenal, gleaned from experience and education – the power of purpose. It was simply a matter of will, and he would succeed. The universe would arrange itself around his quest.

Chapter 5

Once Cruz was outside in the bright light of day, he figured the grip the last hour had had on him would begin to fade, but all he could think of was Una Vida, and Raymond making another teacup for his father's room. He wished there could always be such a simple solution to the broken things of life. There was no way to restore the broken china to its perfect original condition. No way to undo what had been done. But he could, at least, face the break for what it was. He'd justified his absence by telling himself, and Elvira, that he was useless at his mother's bedside; that his true use was to forge ahead with his research, to be able to help her and others like her. Now he knew he was just plain wrong, and that admitting it, at least to himself, was the only way to alleviate the guilt. Admitting it, and pursuing the mystery of Una Vida. The dreams told him that was what his mother would have wanted him to do.

What could he do about identifying the woman who'd contacted him at the cathedral garden? The answer came to him just as he turned the corner to the auditorium hall where Zevie had directed him to his next meeting.

Stompleg. He'd given his card to her. It had to be.

When he entered the auditorium, Cruz was surprised to find only one person awaiting him, his old friend, Morton Friedman. Morton greeted him cheerfully and told Cruz his board of directors had approved the continuation of the sleep-deprivation studies and would ensure further funding.

After a moment, Cruz changed the subject to Alzheimer's and asked Friedman how it was going. Friedman, an impeccable scientist, was a committed Orthodox Jew. His answers to Cruz's "off-the-record" questions always bordered somewhere between the scientific and religious. That had probably been the foundation of their long friendship. Morton was a good person to take a walk with and Cruz had often done that when he was in New York.

When they came to the natural point of ending the conversation, Friedman asked Cruz to close the auditorium door. He changed tone from clinical to engaging.

"What's really on your mind, Alvaro? There's more than just the usual work in your voice."

Though Cruz was scheduled for the rest of the day, he relayed everything to Friedman in the kind of shorthand that only two long-time associates were capable of. He told him about Una Vida, about the woman in the garden, about Stompleg and his dreams of cornfields and banjoes, about the broken teacup and Raymond. Cruz hoped Friedman could offer a coherent explanation for the uncanny experiences he'd been having the past few days.

Friedman responded simply that human life was not like figuring out a math problem. Embedded within it was the mystery of mysteries, and such things don't crack open like a nut.

"We're dealing with beauty and harmony that we have no match for," Friedman said.

"Why keep trying then?"

"Because it's in our very nature to try, however long it takes."

"So I should keep trying, keep investigating her case?" Cruz asked.

"You should try – and *trust*," Friedman replied. "Trust that you and she are *beshert*."

Cruz smiled. He'd always marveled that one Yiddish word could mean providence, fate, destiny, and inevitability – with the underlying meaning that things are meant to be. If meeting Una Vida had been intended, without having a cure for her disease any more than he'd had one for his mother, what could possibly have been the purpose embedded in that "meaningful coincidence?" The expression on Cruz's face was so troubled as the questions ran through his mind that Friedman burst into laughter.

"Who appointed you problem-solver of the universe?" he asked.

Cruz chuckled, and for the moment put it all aside.

*

It was late the next morning by the time Cruz pulled into a parking lot near the old Jax Brewery and walked toward the river again. There was no sign of Stompleg, but he spotted Una Vida walking up from the aquarium. She was a vision with her long gray hair, soft eyes, and ebony skin that was smoother than it should have been at her age. She must have been an incredibly beautiful woman. She still held herself as though she were on stage.

Stompleg had explained that to Cruz during their first encounter: Una Vida radiated an inner glow, even when the stage lights were off her. This time Cruz could see what

Stompleg meant. A powerful aura seemed to emanate from her as she crooned to herself:

> So now, Daddy, here's my plan.
> I ain't gonna play no second fiddle
> I'm used to playing lead...

Cruz recognized it right off as "Ain't Going to Play No Second Fiddle" by Bessie Smith, the unheralded "Empress of the Blues," a beauty to behold in both shape and voice. If he closed his eyes, he could see her there in her 1920s flapper dress and sequined hat – and suddenly Una Vida's voice rang out, brassy and confident, as if she'd been born to sing that song. When she finished, she turned to face the water.

"Bessie Smith?" Cruz asked, as he dropped money into her basket.

She nodded, looking at him blankly.

"The only way to run the demons off."

She rolled her money neatly in a rubber band and placed it in the pocket of her sundress.

"What kind of demons?" Cruz probed.

"Demons is demons, ain't they?"

He moved closer to her.

"Bessie Smith recorded a song with Louis Armstrong called 'St. Louis Blues.' Most folks agree it was the best song recorded in the 1920s."

Una Vida turned to Cruz sharply.

"What you know about Bessie Smith?"

"Not nearly enough," he confessed, pleased by the lucid interaction. "She died some years before I was born, but I know enough to know that her voice helped to shape New Orleans.

"She was a street singer in Chattanooga, Tennessee. She weren't from this here city like King Louis was. And I ain't talking about your King Louis. I'm talking about my King Louis – 'bout ol' Satchmo. Bessie came up that hard way, like we all did. She played with Ma and Pa Rainey's travelin' show. She sang and danced – went on them tours all around to nowhere and in between. Recorded more songs then a queen had diamonds – and she was royalty, ain't no denying that. Louis was the emperor of jazz and Miss Bessie was the empress of the blues."

Una Vida looked right at Cruz then as if she could see through him and belted out a tune that he later learned was a Bessie Smith tune recorded in 1931. She sang it a cappella, but Cruz heard the full wind of the trumpet, trombone, sax, clarinet, and bass in his mind. It was something she did with her voice – something like bringing her gut up into her throat and amplifying it so it floored you when you heard it, literally knocked the wind out of you so that you were never more aware of your beating heart.

People walking by stopped. For a minute there, even Bessie Smith was on the river and stopped to listen. Such was the power of Una Vida's voice. When she finished, Cruz could see that tears were streaming down her face. He looked around and saw that she wasn't the only one – her words had ripped tears out of all the people walking by.

Then he noticed that his own cheeks were moist and dabbed self-consciously at his eyes with the elbows of his jacket.

She walked right up to Cruz as he had moved to her and got in his face.

"Bessie Smith was performing under a big ole kind of a circus tent set up in a farmer's field in Concord, North Carolina. It was sho' hot that night. The band was playin' the blues and Miss Bessie was beltin' 'em out, one after the other – her voice like a trumpet ringin' out in Gideon's name. It was a night of praise and revival. Nobody knew if it was the devil or God that was bein' roused, but they didn't much care – just held on tight to their sweethearts and danced their blues away. Stomped them out like brush fires tryin' to smother your soul and burn the life out of you. You got to play the blues like your hair's on fire if you're gonna help them that need their days in the field exorcised – and that's what the queen was doin' that night: lightin' it up. Those people howled that night like they'd been saved by the finest Baptist preacher ever walked God's green earth."

"How do you know that story?" Cruz asked, mystified.

"Ain't a sharecropper in the South don' know that story by 1928. Story like that get around. Made all our blues stronger. Always knew it was true. Knew it, and knew it fine. My daddy say he ain't believe any woman could save a people, but I knew…knew it wasn't the woman but the blues. And if you singin' the blues real powerful and strong with all your might, you call things up that go beyond man or woman – you call up a spirit that can put a demon down. My daddy didn't want me singin' the blues; said ain't proper a woman be doin' that – ain't proper. Hardly a man I met ever want a woman sing the blues. Maybe that's why I ain't wind up with a man."

"Didn't a man teach you the clarinet?" Cruz asked, testing how logically the memories were linking up in this unexpected spurt of lucidity.

"That man want me to play music, but not blues. That man took me in so long as I follow his ways, kicked me out once I couldn't keep my need of the blues a secret no more. But old Bessie was inside me by then, and these here New Orleans' streets opened up their doors and said, 'Come on in – sing your stuff!' Sho' nuf, that's what I did."

Despite the assault Alzheimer's had mounted on her brain, Una Vida's light was far from being extinguished and drew Cruz in like a moth to flame. He was astonished at her resistance, never having witnessed a woman her age managing to counteract the disease's hold with such a prolonged bout of clarity. His mother certainly had been unable to. Somehow Una Vida was holding back the darkness.

Holding her right hand out in front of her, Una Vida stared into it, as if reading her own palm. She suddenly grabbed it with her left hand and began massaging it, as though trying to rub it clean.

"Blood ain't never gonna come off, much as we scrub."

"Your blood?" Cruz asked.

"Hog's blood."

"What are you referring to?" he asked.

She looked at him to make sure he really wanted to know, and then opened up.

"Killin' day was near Christmas. Weather was cold, and them pigs steamed when you cut 'em open and put they heads to boil in iron pots. Hung them fat hogs upside down from an A-frame post-and-beam rig. Got to drag them hogs over to the rig with a come-along, they so heavy, men sweatin' all over theyselves and all that steam risin' from the slaughtered pigs' open bodies in that freezing weather. The real work began after the man whacked that ole hog on the head with a sledgehammer. We always hoped he got him on the first swing, or else it was a hard one to hold back."

The memories assembled themselves in bits and pieces. One of the emerging memories that somehow held the pieces together went back to Cruz's childhood in Aguilares, when his grandfather Salomon, the father of Aunt Tita, killed a *cochon-a-lait* for the Christmas dinner. The sharp knife, the quick motion toward the neck that his mother prevented him from witnessing, the dinner ceremony afterward, and the toast to his grandfather by everyone.

"With his head cut off, that ole hog's blood drains out like Moses puttin' a plague down on Pharaoh – fill up near everythin' and soak in the ground too – ain't no way to keep on top of it all. We sliced that hog open with the sharpest knife in the lot and grabbed out his guts, cleaned them and separated 'em into the good eatin' parts. Folks got to divvying up them entrails accordin' to who wanted what. Chittlins are the best part, as far as Mama was concerned; she usually tried to get hold of 'em. Mama used to say that some folks were too particular, but not us, we'd eat everythin' but the squeal. And Mama would laugh and laugh."

Una Vida echoed her mama's laugh as though it were reincarnated.

"It weren't often you heard it, but weren't no sweeter sound than that woman laughin', especially when my daddy was bein' sweet on her. She ain't laughed like that in the longest time." Una Vida held her hands out in front of her, took a good look at her palms, and then looked at Cruz as though seeing him for the first time. "Who are you?" she asked. "Why you killin' my pigs?"

Cruz wasn't surprised by her question. It was the exact pattern with Alzheimer's, and he understood it all too well – a sudden and complete disorientation. What got to him most about the diseases he studied was not just the physical suffering they caused, but the havoc they wreaked on human self-respect. He could see the pain in Una Vida's face as she looked at him as if she'd never laid eyes on him.

He processed what was happening inside her brain. Normally we choose a single self from the multiple selves available to us. We construct the illusion of stable meaning, when in reality there is only movement and change and innumerable choices of how to feel and think. At that moment, Una Vida was no longer able to select a consistent self and present it consciously to the world. She was adrift in that pure myriad of mind without a paddle to direct her. One could only guess why she made the choices she made, what triggered her in and out of relatability, both at that moment and before. All the people that had made up her world and the various selves that interacted with it were living only in her brain. The irony was not what little access Una Vida had to them but how much power they had over her.

"Where are you now?" Cruz asked her gently. "How old are you?"

Her eyes widened at his questions, her mix of presence and absence Cruz recognized as a symptom of "moderate to severe Alzheimer's."

"That blood was on your hands even when New Year's come round. We was all just standin' around the iron pots come afternoon, working our magic, rendering fat into lard. We stored our lard in gallon tin buckets and closed them with tight lids. We skimmed out the bubblins off the top and put them aside to make cracklins – skin made real good cracklins – mix it in with cornmeal, flour, and a little baking soda, salt, sugar, and lard and you made yourself a special cornbread. Mama used to slice it thick when it was fresh out the oven and ladle up some field peas that had been simmerin' on the stove since morning. Made a good supper. Bit of cabbage on the side, and was our New Year's good luck supper. 'Bring you health and wealth,' Mama said."

Odd that Iowa has cracklins too; he'd thought they were unique to Louisiana. Una Vida's words broke off and Cruz could sense she was remembering something else – an association that revealed itself like a quick flash of heat lightning across the summer sky. The filters that put each of her cast of characters into proper chronological and spatial place were now crumbled. Had the proper inhibitory neurotransmitters been firing just right, Cruz probably would never have heard the next part. Events and characters had a life of their own, no longer interpreted to suit the needs of the brain's proprietor. They were set free, wanderers in the mind of crumbling walls – the mind of Una Vida. She was not protecting her self-image or anyone else's and she had no ability to control the histrionics. The stage manager had fled the theater.

"Daddy didn't have a New Year after that season. Ain't no way no jake-legger could hold back a 500-pound hog, and Daddy knew it. He just played his blues banjo and sang his songs, rockin' back and forth on a ladder-back chair – seemed to be the only way to calm the tremblin' in his bones."

The banjo again, Cruz thought. Suddenly, his world was filled with banjoes – but what did it mean? Cruz knew that the skeptic's approach would be to connect it with "selective perception." When something makes you aware of banjoes, suddenly the world seems filled with banjoes because you start seeing or hearing them when otherwise you might not have noticed. The skeptic's approach was the one he'd always taken, the only one he'd ever been comfortable with; but he knew clearly somehow that the skeptical approach wasn't operating at that moment.

"It was the first hog-killin' Daddy ever missed. Mama worked harder, trying to make do without help from his big hands. She made ten pans of hog's head cheese and we rendered that lard fast as we could, but folks was still lookin' over at Daddy sittin' on the porch.

"Daddy took to feelin' shame then, I guess. Shame pour over a man like scaldin' water on a yard bird and take the life off him."

Una Vida put her hands back together and started to scrub the way a surgeon does before entering surgery.

Cruz knew better than to ask more questions. He maintained eye contact, hoping she would continue, hoping she would stay with him before the disease took her back to her inner island of oblivion. He lamented the futility of it all, imagined her neurotransmitters translating the neurons' same stories over and over again, like lovers sharing the same cigarette after the same evening in the same small room above the same wrought iron porch in the city of their memory's Vieux Carre. If the memory was pleasant, the affair need never end – the last bite of chocolate never gotten to, its taste lingering like a fog that covered a stream. But if the memory was unpleasant, each moment was excruciating as it played over and over again like a stuck CD. In that sense, Cruz thought, heaven and hell were truly of the mind's making. He was determined to stay with her, to let her know by his presence if by no other means simply that he was listening, simply that he cared.

Una Vida stayed motionless for a full two minutes. Cruz thought sleep had taken her, but she wasn't asleep. The neurons were still sparking. It was as though she'd gone into a trance.

"We scrubbed up with last year's lard soap. Usin' the thing that made us dirty to try and come clean was like usin' the devil to wash our sins away. But Mama said, 'Use what you have, even if it ain't what you need – or understand.'

"I shushed up my two little brothers and the baby girl and put them under the high bed we all sleep on in the back room, then peeked out. Mama and Daddy was fighting, Daddy all wired every which way, shaking and talking crazy, tearin' at his own flesh, screaming how he ain't a man no more. How he just an old jake-legger, no good when he on the stuff and worse when he off it.

"Used to love those homegrown tomatoes. Picked 'em right off the vine and pop 'em in my mouth. All the juice ran down my cheeks and I chewin' on nothin' but sunlight, water, and God. But they'd come and gone out that patch by now. Next I knew, Daddy walked out that way and stood in the empty dirt. Mama begged him not to, but Daddy had

his gun now. Used his left hand to grab hold of his tremblin'
right and steady it long enough to put the gun in his mouth
the way I did a cherry tomato the summer before and pull
the trigger. The red juice that ran down his mouth was blood
this time, and it was made up way beyond God, water, and
sunlight – made up of things I guess he didn't want to let
live on in the world no more."

Tears rolled down Una Vida's cheeks.

"Mama howled like a wounded animal. But then she
saw me standing with my nose to the window and pulled it
together for us children."

Cruz marveled at the rhythmic syntax, which gave him a
glimpse into the brain that had been lost there. Alzheimer's
was the hallmark brain disease, the greatest mystery of them
all, because it crippled its highest function. The brain's cre-
ation of the mind was what made us human. Alzheimer's
was the mind's deconstruction.

"'Nothin' but mud, corn, and cotton in this here place.
Ain't no kind of place to be,' Mama said as she grabbed hold
of me, digging her nails into my arms without realizin' she
was makin' me hurt. Then Mama didn't cry no more; she
packed up a bag with some clothes, Daddy's blues harp, and
some silver. 'You get on out of here now, and don't come
back – get on! New Orleans ain't as far as it feels.' She pulled
me to her hard, nearly breakin' my back with the force of her
love, then pushed me away. 'Go on.' I begged her to let me
stay, 'I'm an Iowa girl,' I sobbed; but she got furious and told
me I wasn't wanted 'round here no more. 'You're Daddy's
girl – you go play the music he was meant to play,' Mama
said. 'I want you to live as free as a bird.'

"I never did say goodbye to the young'ns under that
bed. Mama held my face to the door with her strong hands,
makin' sure I didn't look back. Didn't want me makin' the

64

same mistake Lot's wife did – and I ain't never look back since."

"And what year is it now?" Cruz pressed.

"1933, I told you. Mama was standin' there sayin', 'I'm sorry you ain't never learned to read and write, but you can play that thing and sing real pretty, too. If a woman can play music in New Orleans, they say she free. So get on now! Don't be burdened with this whole mess no more.' She pushed me out that door. I made my way to the highway and hitched a ride all the way to New Orleans."

"How old were you?" Cruz asked.

"Fifteen. Grown woman mostly, though. Long time out of school."

"You didn't learn to read and write in school?"

"Never thought much about it. Them letters was always backwards. Couldn't hardly see nothin' those teachers was tellin' me was in those books. When I tried to write things, got a whippin' for havin' my letters turned upside and around. Teachers said I was dumb. Most folks went to school up to sixth grade, but they figured it wasn't no use with me. Daddy taught me on his harmonica and his songs, even how to draw the likeness of a man. He made me paint from the dye of a plant – Daddy knew all them country tricks. After a while, I was paintin' folks so true, nearly scared them to death. Like I'd put a mirror in front of 'em they weren't ready to see."

She trailed off, suddenly seeming weary and frail. Cruz didn't want to push her too far, too fast.

"Are you hungry?" he asked her.

"Sure is," she smiled. "I'm eatin' for two now."

Taking her by the arm, Cruz walked Una Vida toward the Quarter. She quickly began talking again, though where she was in time he could never be sure. They stopped at Maspero's, New Orleans' most popular sandwich parlor for those who don't feel like a muffaletta. The place served tasty food and gave you way too much of it. You washed it down with a nice glass of local Abita beer for two dollars and felt at home. With no air conditioning inside, the windows on the street opened into a dark wood space that boasted an old bar in front and wooden tables and chairs that hadn't changed in thirty years. Cruz and Una Vida were seated by a heavily tattooed, stubbly-faced doorman. A waitress with dark hair, overflowing breasts, and short legs quickly made her appearance, dropping silverware rolled in paper napkins onto the table and two yellow-tinted glasses of tap water with ice.

Cruz ordered roast beef po'boys, fully dressed – an overflowing sandwich on soft French bread. Louisiana was the only place in the world Cruz had known where you ordered a roast beef sandwich in gravy and it came dressed with mayo, lettuce, and tomato – right there on top of the gravy. Twenty years ago, he'd thought it an outrage; over time, he'd acquired a taste for it. Apparently, Una Vida didn't object to the mixture either. She was wolfing hers down, along with a side of fries and a Barq's.

"Thank you for buyin' me this meal, sir. I was looking for a gig to play tonight so's I could get some money for my baby and me; was gonna hold out to eat 'til after the show. But you just saved me the trouble. My baby thanks you, too. I can feel it happy as can be in there."

Cruz, his hunger quenched for the moment, interrupted the verbal riff that had continued nearly nonstop since they'd left the levee. He was wondering which incarnation of Una Vida he was now talking to.

"How old are you?"

"Nineteen," she answered immediately. "I play clarinet in a jazz band, sing the blues, too. Not very good yet, but I'm workin' on it."

"And you live alone?"

"Do now. Since he kicked me out."

"Why?" Cruz wanted to know.

"Said he didn't get me those lessons so I could go play jazz. He wanted me to learn to play in an orchestra 'stead with those 'street hoodlums,' like he calls 'em. I told him there ain't no orchestra no more and never was for a girl like me. He said there would be an orchestra and I ought to save myself for it and not sell my talent for dimes on the street. I told him jazz was the only music I wants to play, no matter how much his wife and little girl cried over it. Creole man got lots of pride in this city. Lotta pride."

"Do they know about the baby?" Cruz asked.

"No, sir, not a thing. No reason to tell 'em, neither. Can't never go back there 'cause I ain't never gonna stop playing jazz and learning to sing the blues like Bessie. Her voice turned the devil to dust. Ain't no orchestra can do that."

Cruz sat eating his roast beef and talking as though they were both right in the moment of something that had oc-curred nearly sixty years ago. He asked what her real name was, but Una Vida only answered that she had to get back to her show and drank down the last gulp of her root beer from the tinted yellow glass.

"I need to find some reeds," she said, standing up abruptly.

Cruz stood, too, and signaled for the check. He was glad to see Una Vida looking stronger after the meal. He asked where she bought her reeds. Without answering, she took him by the hand.

When they got to Chartres Street, Una Vida let go of his hand. She held her clarinet to her lips and began to play a tune. But it was off.

Cruz realized she was proving something. He watched her take out the flimsy falling-apart reed.

"I been telling this woman I need reeds but don't have no money," she explained. "Can you help?"

"You have money," Cruz said, pulling the wad of rolled up cash from her pocket and placing it in her hand.

"Best manager in all New Orleans, ain't you, John? Keepin' my money safe for me like that. Why don't you take me on to that music store uptown, then back over to the inn so's I can get rested up before the tour tomorrow – lotsa cities to travel on that broken-down ole bus, and a woman can't even stop to get herself a decent cup of coffee in most of 'em." Una Vida put her clarinet in her case and took Cruz's arm. "You still drivin' that old gray thing of yours?"

"I got something new," Cruz thought quickly. "Want to take a look?"

She laughed and slapped him on the back.

"Making fine money off us, ain't you, John?"

*

The music store on Broadway was about to close, but they caught the twenty-something college kid just as he was about to cash out his register. When Cruz told him it would just be a minute, the kid acted annoyed, but acquiesced. Inside, Cruz asked him for the reeds. As an expert talking to a novice can sometimes do, the kid made Cruz feel silly as he named all the varieties of reeds sold in the store. Cruz told him he'd better get the clarinet from the car.

When he came back, Una Vida had come out of her temporarily passive gaze and was lecturing to the boy.

"I know what kind of music you listenin' to on that radio. That Benny Goodman's a real good clarinet player. He's super good on the National Biscuit Company's *Let's Dance* show. I listen myself. But let me tell you something. When Benny Goodman was first comin' up in that tenement, he learned right quick that the only place a Jewish boy gonna learn to play real jazz is to make his way out of Brooklyn and get on up to Harlem. Didn't matter 'bout segregation to Benny Goodman – what he cared 'bout was the music, and he wanted to watch and learn. When he finally got this radio show some months back, a friend of his told him that if he was to do it right and keep the interest of the audience comin' back every week, he'd have to get a better arrangement.

"So he went to the best arranger in Harlem that he could get – Fletcher Henderson. Henderson sold Goodman songs and gave him what was called his 'Harlem Book,' with all them old tunes arranged in a new way that could really swing. Goodman paid dear for it and made his career on it. Now most folk still think us uneducated jazz musicians can't read or write music. They think some smart uppity folks are writin' music for us jazz folk to play and we just memorize it. Couldn't be further from the truth. On the radio in 1934, it's Benny Goodman, a poor Jewish boy from a tenement in Brooklyn, playing the songs written for him by Fletcher Henderson, a poor black man calls Harlem home. Boy like you wouldn't believe that, would you?"

"I believe it," the teenager said, spellbound.

"Well, good. It's good you believe."

He helped Una Vida find her reeds. She screwed a new one on and played the boy a Fletcher Henderson tune called "The Unknown Blues," a quick tune. As she played, Cruz thought he could hear a bit of Henderson's piano in the background.

The boy named the tune right off, then told them he was a music major at U.N.O. He asked Una Vida if she might come to his jazz class to play and speak to them.

"My professor would be honored," he added.

"Ain't gonna let me in no college."

Una Vida brushed the boy off and made her way out the door.

Cruz would later confirm that everything Una Vida told the boy that day was true. In fact, Goodman had invited Henderson to join his orchestra and play alongside him, and they played together until 1947. Henderson came to New York from Atlanta in 1920. He had graduated the University of Atlanta with a degree in chemistry and had gone to New York to do graduate work and land a job. He found that most doors of academia were closed to him, so he fell back on his music skills and played piano, arranged music, and led a band at the best clubs in Harlem. For a long while, his star trumpet player was Louis Armstrong.

Cruz knew it was time to take Una Vida back to the levee and for him to leave for home. He had a vague sense that he was forgetting something. The break in routine was playing tricks on his mind. When he got them back to the car, Una Vida laid her head back on the seat and fell asleep almost immediately. Cruz switched his cell phone on and waited as it buzzed, alerting him to all the messages he'd missed. He quickly discovered what he'd forgotten: Elvira was heading down to the Quarter in her own car so they could meet at Preservation Hall. He looked at his watch. He'd just have time to make it.

As they parked in a thirty-minute spot near the levee, Una Vida woke up.

"You be sure to stop by my place so I can pick up the clothes I need for the tour."

"Where is your place?"

The look in her eye told him she was in some other cave than the present.

"915 Royal Street," she said with a dreamy note in her voice.

The address sounded vaguely familiar, but Cruz couldn't envision that block of Calle Real. Before he could interrogate her further, a shout distracted him. Stompleg had spotted them getting out of the car and was hobbling toward them, every bone in his body expressing agitation.

"Where've y'all been?" he asked, his voice riddled with anxiety.

"I took her to buy some reeds," Cruz explained, holding up the bag from the music store.

Stompleg frowned at Una Vida and zipped open her clarinet case. It was filled with new reeds.

"She always asking for reeds, spends every dollar she gets her hands on buying more. That's why I worry 'bout her starvin' to death. Got enough reeds to last a whole other lifetime."

Of course, Cruz was not surprised. With her brain flitting from year to year, it would have been a miracle if she could have kept track of her belongings at any given time.

Stompleg took Una Vida by the hand.

"I been gone less than forty-eight hours and you out there takin' advantage of the good doctor," he admonished her.

She didn't respond. Her face was blank as she escaped into caves he could not reach.

"I was worried Jessica got to you," Stompleg said to Cruz. "Amitė warned me I shouldn't have gotten you involved with her."

Cruz suddenly realized that Jessica must have been the name of the woman who had lured him to the cathedral.

"You gave someone named Jessica my card?"

Stompleg's guilty look told Cruz all he needed to know.

"If you don't trust her, why'd you hook her up with me?"

"That was before I talked to Amitė," he shrugged. Then his tone got defensive. "I can't take care of her forever. Ain't got the means or the know-how. Besides, got my own life to hold together." He snorted. "I ain't doin' that good a job on that, either." Stompleg told Cruz he'd made a quick trip to check out the Artists' Home. "That girl just read the medicine cards for me when I couldn't find Una Vida," he pressed on. "She been readin' the medicine cards for near twenty-five years. Grew up on the reservation in Pine Ridge…Ogallala Sioux. She read my spread when I told her I'd given Jessica your card. The raven came up, and I believe the deep healin' represented there is you, a professional who can help Una Vida. But the rabbit card came up, too, and it represents fear. That's Jessica."

Cruz remembered thinking that Jessica, as she darted into the crowd to escape him, had reminded him of a scared rabbit.

"She can scare a man away from doin' the good he needs to do. And you wouldn't be the first scared away by a beauty like that. So you be real careful. Amité's cards don't lie."

Una Vida was sagging. Cruz scolded himself for ignoring her.

"You'd better get her home," he said. "She's had an exhausting day." Then he added, "She said she lives on Royal."

Stompleg cackled. "Una Vida says lotsa things got no bearin' on reality."

He told Cruz that he might find Jessica in Jackson Square or off Bienville, where she sometimes sold her pots.

"She's a potter?"

"When she gets high, she hawks these weird-shaped pots – the kind you can't drink out of cuz they'd probably break apart. I knew her back when she worked the club on Bourbon; we all did." Stompleg paused, feeling that he'd sufficiently made his point.

"Thanks for your concern, I appreciate your – "

Stompleg pressed harder when he heard the tone of distant formality in Cruz's voice, as though he didn't want to hear what was being said.

"Addicts lie," Stompleg said. "They're crafty – have to be. Nobody knows that better'n me, and a pretty woman like that – forget it – no tellin' how much money she's taken people for by sellin' her sob story and those crazy coffee cups."

"What's her last name?"

"I'm sure she's had a dozen," Stompleg said. "Who knows? She's a lost soul. I was saved, but most people out here, they don't get saved. Jessica never did."

Cruz shook his head.

"Maybe she's still working on it. Maybe you're meant to have a hand in it."

Stompleg laughed.

"Don't think so. I was saved by the blues, and that's why Una Vida's comfortable with me. Jessica will never have that."

He made the last statement sound like an initiation into a secret society, but Parker would tell Cruz much the same thing: the Delta blues saved many a person from the hardship of their own memories. People have theorized that the blues came about as a kind of spell – a mesmerizing ritual act that could heal the singer, the players, and those listening in the call-and-response fashion not so different from the revivalist churches that dotted the Delta. The difference was that there was no doctrine to believe, only a rhythm to feel. It has been said that to sing the blues is to purge – to cleanse oneself from the day's hardship – to practice the art of forgetting pain.

As Branford Marsalis expressed it, "The blues are about freedom."

If singing and playing the blues could save a man from the agony of a life of sharecropping, Stompleg argued, it could certainly save one skinny ex-heroine addict who learned to play behind the bars of Angola.

Cruz had no doubt about the power of the blues and he was glad for Stompleg, but wondered why potters couldn't have their own access to salvation.

Chapter 6

$\mathcal{A}$s the mood of the jazz began to settle him into his chair, Cruz was grateful he had insisted on planning this evening with Elvira. Preservation Hall was one of the oldest, most run-down, and organically beautiful jazz clubs in New Orleans. He had tried to get her to meet him for dinner before the show at Rio Mar, their favorite Spanish-Mediterranean restaurant, but had gratefully settled for meeting her there at eight o'clock when she said she needed to stop at Malta Park after work. He was thrilled that she greeted him with a warm kiss, which told him she was pleased to be out on a weeknight with her husband for an occasion that had nothing to do with work or out-of-town guests.

They paid their five-dollar entry fee and took their places among the crowded bodies in the back of the hall. The Hall was adorned with decrepit wooden benches, a few ceiling fans in front for the band members, and painted pictures framed without glass or lighting. Bessie Smith, Ella Fitzgerald, Satchmo, and the rest of the crew peered out dimly from the dark paint of the past. Their images were the holy family of this church. The Hall could have fallen apart at any minute, but was held together by the will of jazz and the people who spawned it. The musicians in front had no special lighting or costumes, no microphones or any sort of amplification equipment. Cruz was always struck by the utter nakedness. The players who performed in this unencumbered space had only the air in their lungs and the instruments at their lips to communicate their message. No ambience, no pyrotechnics, no set designer, no sound man, nothing to weave the audience into their magic spell – just breath, instruments, and love.

No question, the trumpet player was phenomenal. Not only was his playing uplifting, but he also cajoled the audience into participation and exuberance. By tradition, the trumpeter at Preservation Hall was in the center and acted as band leader. Tonight, he didn't disappoint. The audience was captivated. As the show went on, some of the most beautiful melodic harmonies that Cruz had ever heard touched his soul. He could have sworn it was something completely nature's own and eternally pure, the sound was ringing out from the man-made clarinet. The man blowing was close to Cruz's age. Cruz didn't know a thing – didn't *need* to know a thing – about his personality, his life, his memories, or his mind; but he was grateful to him because the man took Cruz out of himself, into the eternal moment. Even the trumpet player looked to the clarinet for guidance throughout the show. The blower led the band, not with the force of personality or charisma that the trumpet player displayed, but with his playing: it spoke for itself, out on the edge of invention and risk. The clarinet's music transported Cruz, Elvira, and the audience to a place of its choosing, a place where they checked their individual selves at the door and participated in the communion of jazz – and followed as willingly as the

76

children of Hamlin. The mystic clarinet player did not have to wait 3,000 years to arrive at the human center of meaning. He had arrived there that night and took Cruz with him.

*

After the show, Elvira pulled Cruz close as they walked through the intoxicated maelstrom of Bourbon Street. They walked in silence, neither of them ready to break the spell. In years past, they'd often held each other this way after church, but something else had been touched tonight. Cruz had been transported. He was feeling forgiven. He was forgiving the mysterious Jessica for running away before he could learn anything from her. Everything had been swept away by the music.

They had walked almost as far as Plaza de Armas before Cruz realized they were still holding hands. If Elvira was forgiving him, maybe he was even capable of forgiving himself.

"Let's find Handsome John," he said, "and take a carriage tour of the Quarter."

Elvira smiled her agreement.

"What's gotten into you, suggesting something so touristy?"

"Don't discourage me; I'm learning to follow the music," he said.

Her only answer was a gentle squeeze of his hand as they walked to Decatur and looked for the driver among the carriages lined up in front of Jackson Square. Handsome John spotted them first.

"I see you're a man of your word," he laughed. "Hop on up."

Cruz explained to Elvira that he'd told the driver he would take a rain check.

"How many shifts do you work?" he asked the man.

Handsome John's laugh was contagious.

"Boss, my life's one big shift. Ain't nobody to spell me. If I'm not drivin', I'm not makin' money."

He tipped his hat to emphasize his point. Cruz noticed he was wearing a fresh carnation.

The entire French Quarter comprised only thirteen by six blocks, but a carriage tour for two still cost fifty dollars. Handsome John started by talking about water.

"The average height of the city of New Orleans is 6.5 feet below sea level," he said, his voice taking on an experienced sing-song. "The average height of the French Quarter is five feet above sea level on account of the bend of the river building up sediment and dumping it on the land that came to make up the Quarter."

He went on as if they were tourists, and Cruz opened his mouth to tell him he could skip the narration – until he saw Elvira's expression and thought better of it. Why not put himself into the ferryman's hands? Wasn't that part of "going with the flow?"

"The city has twenty-two pumping stations because low as we are, drainage doesn't happen naturally. If Lake Ponchartrain floods, we're all in trouble and have to evacuate – the city has elaborate evacuation systems, so don't worry," Handsome John assured them the way locals do wide-eyed tourists.

From the twinkle in his eye, Cruz surmised that John was as aware as they were that they were residents, not tourists, but he seemed to be enjoying giving them their money's worth. So they would enjoy it, too, despite the vague premonition caused by Handsome John's words. The old driver pointed out the Faulkner House in Pirate's Alley, where Cruz had tried to follow Jessica into the crowd.

"That's where William Faulkner stayed when he wrote his first novel in 1925, *Soldier's Pay.*"

Una Vida hadn't yet arrived in New Orleans at that point, Cruz thought, but jazz was already at its pinnacle.

Jackson Square, where people gathered to cavort and to publicly execute, was the center of the Quarter. The square was renamed in the 1840s for Andrew Jackson as tribute to his heroism in the battle of Orleans during the war of 1812. The square had been called the Place d'Armes by the French. Jackson Square was landscaped in a sun pattern, with garden paths moving out from its centerpiece statue of Andrew Jackson on horseback.

"Some old timers and residents of the Quarter," John explained, "still call it *Vieux Carre*, 'Old Square.'"

As they rode up Chartres, Handsome John talked about the streets having been dirt and mud up until 1948.

"They were breeding grounds for disease. No pumping stations then, and all the rain just sat still in these old carriage ways. Yellow fever took root and the epidemic spread. The church banned open caskets and stopped having services for the dead inside the cathedral. In 1853 alone, 10,000 people died of the fever."

As Handsome John drove them past the Ursuline convent, his mule, Red, started to slow down considerably. Without his whip, he bunched up his brown leather reins a little and tried to persuade Red to pick up the pace, but she didn't feel it a bit and crawled along at her own pace. Elvira and Cruz didn't mind. They eventually made it up to Gallatin Street and to what Handsome John called the Little Italy of New Orleans. A walking tour passed by, the New Orleans haunted tour, with guides dressed like quasi-vampires.

"I hate to see that," Handsome John said. "People getting ripped off with a bunch of lies. At least let's tell the truth and not spread legends around and make a buck off it," he said passionately to Elvira. He then shouted directly to the crowd, "Ain't no such thing as vampires, never were. You know who the vampires are? Me and you!"

He tried to speed away without much luck.

"Get up, Red. Come on, get up there!" He turned around to Elvira and Cruz. "Sorry about that. I just don't like seeing folk deceived and payin' good money to be done that way."

He drove Red on toward Bourbon Street. For a moment, Cruz was sorry he'd picked Handsome John, but then Elvira pulled him toward her excitedly.

"This is so much fun!" she laughed.

"I'm glad," he said, squeezing her hand. "Not the best place to get back in synch with my wife again," he added, "with all the chatter, but – "

Just as they turned the corner onto Orleans, Cruz spotted Jessica staring at them from the doorway of a sleazy bar. She looked transformed, from the warm earth of which he'd glimpsed her at their encounter into the cold steel of a stranger. She was standing at the doorway, half-clothed to lure men in, as was the custom around Bourbon Street. He saw her and didn't want to believe it, but his brain had registered it. Before he could catch Elvira's attention, Jessica saw that she'd been spotted and turned away.

"Was that woman in the doorway a hooker?" Cruz asked John, keeping his tone even.

Handsome John shrugged, as though the question wasn't worth answering, and continued with his monologue.

"Since y'all went to Preservation Hall this evenin', the question I thought you were going to ask is how is this all related to jazz?"

"That was my next question," Elvira smiled.

"I thought so," John nodded.

Cruz knew what he was about to say.

"They called the women of the old Storyville establishments 'Jezebels.' All the great ones got their start playing music in the bordellos of Storyville: Louis Armstrong, Jelly Roll Morton, Duke Ellington – they all played here. These places were known for the music, fancy bars, and for the way the girls danced to this wild new sound. People called it Jezebel music. After a while it got shortened to Jez music, then eventually jazz as the music tried to separate itself from the world that spawned it."

They were circling back to their starting point when Handsome John said, "I'll tell y'all one more thing about Storyville that most people don't know, but I always found interesting. See where we are now? We're several blocks from the entrance to Storyville and not far from the waterfront. Sailors used to come off these ships with money in their pockets and a plan to head down to Storyville, but they'd usually stop off in one of the many waterfront bars to have just one drink. Anybody knows there's no such thing as one drink in a bar, so one turns into two and next thing you know, they're leaving the bar with a pretty good one tied on. First thing they see down here by the waterfront when they come out is the "mattress girls" – prostitutes walking around with mattresses on their backs. Kind of like traveling salesmen. These mattress girls, who were lower class self-employed free agents, unlike the Storyville girls who were on contract with the bordellos, started takin' business away from the bordellos. The Storyville girls got mad and started coming down here and fightin' the mattress girls."

Cruz finally spoke, "I have a question for you."

"Go ahead," Handsome John said as he tried to move Red along.

"You know Bourbon Street pretty well."

"More than I want to," John said. "What's on your mind?"

"The club we passed on the tour, the one I asked about. You said it wasn't that bad."

"No, as far as the clubs on Bourbon go, that one's respectable. Why?"

"I think that girl I asked you about works there," Cruz said.

Both Elvira and Handsome John looked at him.

"Whatever you say," Handsome John clucked to Red. "Don't make me no never mind."

"Do you know her?" Cruz continued.

Then he looked at Elvira, whose face showed her curiosity at her husband's line of questioning. Handsome John seemed to flinch.

"You *are* from N'awlins?" For the first time, Handsome John's voice held a note of uncertainty.

"I live here, if that's what you mean. Do you know her?" Cruz raised his voice, growing impatient.

"What is she to y'all, then?"

"She's a friend."

Handsome John's shoulders slumped, but his voice was flat as he answered, "Sure I know her. Used to, anyway... haven't seen her work any of these clubs in a long time. Most of these clubs here aren't that far away from the Storyville days; it's just a hell of a whole lot sleazier now. The VIP rooms in the upstairs of those clubs are where the big money is for the girls. Anything goes up there, but nobody talks about it. Cops look the other way. Last I heard, that girl was sculpting clay or something like that, though. How long have you known her?" John's voice showed an odd mixture of disdain and concern, something Cruz couldn't place.

Cruz reassured Elvira with a glance that said he'd explain all when they were alone.

A carriage moving toward them suddenly veered so close that Cruz thought they were going to collide. Then he saw the veer was intentional as the driver pulled up alongside Handsome John with a long red whip in his hand.

"Drop this on your graveyard tour, did you? That's bad luck, John – or were you waving it at the vampires again?" the other driver smiled.

John regained his whip gladly, and Cruz suspected his next tour would be much quicker than theirs was.

They were proceeding as if nothing had happened, though John flicked his whip at Red as they approached Royal Street and Red responded immediately as if he was grateful to return to his masochistic routine.

"Ain't nothing wrong with her, really. Don't worry about her. She's a good kid."

He brushed his eye with his sleeve.

Handsome John's delivery became more rapid as though with his whip back he realized he needed to speed the economy along. He began his Royal Street spiel.

"On the right up yonder," he said, "is one of the most romantic buildings in New Orleans. It's called the Cornstalk Inn."

*

Cruz's attention was riveted on the building with the same instant import as the feeling that the banjo chords on the levee had induced. What he didn't notice as he studied the green wrought iron fence and the yellow-frame Victorian bed and breakfast was that Elvira was also riveted.

"I love the story of this place…the fact that somebody would care so much," Elvira said, referring to the story that the owner's wife had been from Iowa and that he'd built the green cornstalk fence to remind her of her home.

"Stop the carriage, please," Cruz said.

Handsome John ignored him for a moment.

"Got to keep movin'," he answered.

"No. Stop immediately."

Cruz took a $100 bill from his billfold and waved it toward the old driver. His eyes were focused on the address above the front door of the Cornstalk Inn: 915–915 Royal Street, the address Una Vida had given him as her "home" that afternoon at the levee.

"Yassir," Handsome John intoned. "Money always talks, suh."

Elvira looked surprised as Cruz stepped lightly from the carriage and offered her his hand to dismount. They waved as they watched the carriage ride away empty.

"I didn't ask him about Una Vida," Cruz said.

"You can ask him in the morning," Elvira spoke his thought.

Then her husband said something she hadn't heard from him in thirty-two years: "Let's not go to work tomorrow."

Her shock was as great as if her husband had just told her he could fly.

"We couldn't – " she stammered. "The research team, the results tomorrow, your trip to Spain, the – "

She was obviously trying to protect him from himself, thinking he'd regret it and work double over the weekend.

"What's life if you can't take a day off once in a while?" Cruz said. "We'll stay in the Quarter tonight rather than head back up town."

Elvira searched for something in her purse. Oddly, the hair on her arms was standing up.

"I was wondering when we would use this," she said, her voice trembling slightly as she pulled out an envelope.

"What's that?" Cruz asked.

"You really don't remember, do you?"

Cruz tried to recall if he'd told her about the cornfield dreams in detail. He'd intended to tell her everything on the carriage ride, not having foreseen Handsome John's garrulity.

"We bid on a night here at that silent auction about six

months ago to benefit Malta Park," Elvira reminded him. "You told me to give it to Chela and Diego for a gift, but I decided to hold onto it for us – some special occasion."

"You aren't going to believe the story I have to tell you – and this is the exact place where it was meant to be told," he said excitedly.

"Of course I'm going to believe it. You've become a lightning rod of coincidence lately."

She kissed his cheek when they reached the front gate. He asked Elvira what he could have built her to remind her of Argentina. She didn't answer, just taking his hand and leading him inside the gate.

They glided through the foyer to the bell stand at the end of the hall. They could see through the door that the innkeeper was watching the last few minutes of the Hornets game, the first of the season for New Orleans' new basketball team. For New Orleans to have a basketball team with a name anything other than the Jazz seemed absurd, but such was the way of politics and commerce – the Jazz ended up in Utah.

Cruz showed the certificate for the free room and the man got busy processing the information with one eye on the game and one on the paperwork.

"Do you have luggage?" he asked routinely.

A commercial was just starting, so they had his full attention.

"No," Elvira offered, "no luggage. I was going to ask you if you have extra toiletries down here – maybe some toothbrushes and toothpaste, a corkscrew. A good bottle of red wine you can add to our tab?"

The man turned to look at them now, scanning quickly, then gave them toothbrushes, toothpaste, room keys, quick instructions about breakfast, a bottle of Pinot Noir from the Willamette Valley of Oregon that he grabbed from a wine rack and reverently wiped clear of dust – that would probably cost them dearly – and a corkscrew. They thanked him, just as the interminable commercials gave way to the game again.

"What's the score?" Cruz asked as the man walked away.

"92–78. Looks like New Orleans is going to start the year on a winning note."

They walked the two flights to their room, closed the door, and laughed like children. Elvira told Cruz she hadn't seen him this way since they were dating.

Cruz opened the wine with a playful flourish. Elvira took the two glasses covered with paper hats that sat by the bathroom sink and brought them out to the balcony. He remembered thinking at the auction that they'd never use the room, and now he wondered whether the auction prize had been what started him dreaming of cornfields.

But when he opened the French doors of their suite and walked out onto the balcony over the courtyard, he knew that it hadn't been like any other donation. It was *beshert*. Kismet. He still didn't understand what it all meant, but for the moment he didn't care. The wrought iron cornstalks, row on row in almost military precision glistening dark green in the moonlight, mesmerized him and took him to that strange place between consciousness and unconsciousness. The air was cool and the moon was full. It was past midnight. Their bodies and minds were beginning to relax, even more so after the first glass of wine passed their lips. All they heard was the sound of the large cast iron fountain in the courtyard.

They kissed in the moonlight on the balcony with the soothing sound of the fountain below. It was comforting not to have any baggage. Elvira put her hand in Cruz's and grew steadily quieter as she studied her husband for a sign.

"What is it, Alvaro?" she finally asked.

He took a deep breath, inhaling the fragrance of the honeysuckle entwined around the balcony railing.

"I'd rather die than live without you," he said, surprising even himself with the force of his words.

By answer, she stood on her tiptoes and kissed him. "I do love you, Alvaro. Despite everything."

"But can you ever forgive me?"

"I don't need to forgive you. You need to forgive yourself." She watched a perplexed look capture his face. "There's no hurry," she chuckled gently. "It will happen when you're ready."

"Maybe when I feel I've earned it."

"Maybe."

"I really did love her," he said.

"I know you did."

"I just couldn't handle what had happened to her."

"You took it as a personal insult."

He realized she was exactly right. Suddenly that rainy day in Rome came back to him so vividly that he winced. Elvira's voice across the cell phone was as clear as if she were in the next room.

"Your mother is failing. Fast. You need to come home."

"But I just arrived here. My talk is in the morning."

"She's your mother," was Elvira's only response.

That was undeniable: his only mother, who would live, and die, only once.

"Is there any hope at all?" he found himself asking – a question that, looking back on it, revealed the coolly clinical logic of his own obsession.

"No," she'd answered. "You'd better hurry. She may not last another day."

Like dominoes falling one after another, his thoughts processed to their logical conclusion. If there was nothing to be done, then why need he rush back? Wasn't it a man's highest purpose in life to focus on what he *could do* and let go of things beyond his power to affect? If he rushed back and got there too late, he would have shirked his duty to learn more about the brain by presenting his conclusions the next morning and receiving the critique of his most distinguished peers. Either way – even if he arrived before she breathed her last – she would not know who he was. And, truthfully, that had been, he admitted now, what he felt to be the greatest betrayal of all: a man's mother, not recognizing the son she'd given birth to.

Like a petulant schoolboy denied his request to borrow the family car, the adult Alvaro Cruz was simply, and deeply, angry at his mother for abandoning him. And without an ounce of human kindness he had, in the years during which she had deteriorated before his eyes, rejected her. How could he ever forgive himself for that?

"Don't be so hard on yourself," he heard Elvira saying, as though she could read his mind.

And he was back on the balcony of the Cornstalk Inn with her, listening to the sound of the water cascading in a way that became predictable after a while and provided a mesmerizing comfort that he had no right to enjoy. Cruz stared at Elvira without saying anything at first.

"Tell me," she prodded.

He finally coughed out the whole story. He put her hand to his face and stared into her eyes. He told her everything – first haltingly and with parts held back, then like the flurry in which it had been happening, with all the attending feelings and thoughts. He even told her of the dreams and about how he knocked over Handsome John and caused him to bleed in the maze. About how the corn wouldn't stop growing and would eventually cover up this very balcony if he didn't get to the heart of the mystery.

He also told her about Jessica, and as he started to talk about the coincidence of both Jessica and Raymond being potters, Elvira's eyes filled with tears. Her brother-in-law had been a potter in Argentina twenty-five years ago. But he had been an activist as well, and joined the ranks of the hundreds of thousands of "the disappeared ones" – *los desapacidos* – never to be heard from again.

"His hands were so beautiful," Elvira finally said.

It was all flooding back for Cruz now: Roberto and all the others. He thought of Una Vida and the caves of memory that she spilled out to him without knowing who he was. Maybe before that she hadn't thought of the jake-leg in years, hadn't recalled the sweet tomato and the bitter bullet.

Cruz was struck by his own willful forgetting, how effective it had been to keep focused on the hopeful and the positive; he spoke to his wife of Roberto and little details he remembered about his mother. The time with Elvira became a midnight of forgiveness and rendezvous. They dreamed of Argentina before the war, when everything had been sweet and peaceful and right.

Elvira listened intently as she savored her wine and told him that sometimes reality and dreams needed to approach each other more closely than usual to put things on the track they were destined to be on. That sometimes your conscious brain can't do it alone, but recognizes that it has the power of the unconscious at its beck and call, and the good sense to become open to its influence. She understood what her husband had been struggling with; his desire to "connect the dots" so the world of rationality he presided over like a guru coincided perfectly with the transcendent world that left rationality behind. She understood why he'd remained in Rome, even though she didn't approve.

"No one has ever pieced it *all* together," she reminded him. "That doesn't mean the two worlds don't coexist."

She told Cruz she'd read that the ancient Greeks visited "incubation temples," where they made an offering to sleep there for the night and under the patronage of the goddess of sleep and the priestess in charge of the temple, incubated a dream that would bring them the divine inspiration they required to go on with their lives.

"Will you be my priestess tonight – *and* my goddess?"

She took his hand and led him to the bed.

*

"Did you dream?" Elvira asked him in the morning, when she came out to the balcony.

Cruz was already staring at the courtyard fountain as if entranced.

"I did," he said. "How about you?"

Her musical laughter echoed in the tiny courtyard.

"I'm afraid I slept like the dead. All the dream power went to you."

"You're a good goddess," Cruz said, smiling at the memory of the night before and kissing her tenderly.

"Are you going to tell me about it?"

"Over coffee," he answered. "In your favorite place."

Since their arrival in New Orleans twenty-four years ago, Elvira had never gotten over her love for the Café du Monde, at the start of the French Market, across from Jackson Square. It was late morning by the time they got there, and Cruz could see that the green-and-white striped awning still had not been replaced – a fixture to remind him of the first time they'd been escorted to that traditional coffee house for café au lait and beignets. The awning had just been installed the day before their first visit.

That morning, as on that day so long ago, an Asian waiter appeared almost immediately at their table in a white uniform that also hadn't changed since the café's opening –

sporting an oval-shaped paper hat that bore the green-lettered Café Du Monde insignia on it. Cruz flashed another memory, of his son Nicolas wanting one of those hats when he was a boy. He bought him one at the gift shop and Nicolas wore it proudly as he drank his milk at a table not far from the one where he and Elvira were sitting. It was amazing how little effort it took to please a child, Cruz thought.

The waiter had brought two ice waters with him, along with napkins; he set them down and stood ready to take their order. A small street jazz band was playing for tips just beyond the café. The café was wide open to the street, and on sunny days, sitting outside was pleasant. In the dead of summer you sat, drank ice coffee – extra ice – and perspired.

When the beignets arrived, Cruz saw that the dough had been fried to perfection: crisp on the outside, soft on the inside, and covered in a thick layer of powdered sugar. Some people said that beignets had been invented there. The key to eating them was in trying not to inhale as you brought the pastry to your mouth. If you did, even in the slightest, the powdered sugar went up your nose and into your throat – making you cough wildly. Since they didn't know the secret, tourists were dead giveaways.

After their first practiced bites, Cruz told Elvira about the vivid dream he'd experienced at their Cornfield Incubation Temple:

I was standing in a freshly mowed field. I could smell the grass and see purple and red wildflowers off to the edge. I wanted to stay in the field, but I looked up and saw Jessica. She had come out of nowhere. She took my arm and led me to a stand of corn.

"Do you want to come in?" she asked.

"I usually stay here," I said, breathing in the smell of something fresher and incredibly pure.

"But the music is in here," she told me, pointing to the corn.

She ran into an open path in the cornfield and I followed; this time, I didn't hesitate. I was trying to keep up, when blues music gave way to jazz, and I couldn't hear her footsteps over the banjo music.

I quickly realized that I was in a maze – "a maze of maize," I remember thinking, with surprise – and the faster I ran, the more lost I was, the more out of breath. I longed for the spacious field of moments before, but it was nowhere to be seen. When I was in the middle of the maze, it started to grow and multiply – the stalks of corn began to morph; they looked like dentritic neuronal arbors. The growing field was taking over everything and the only way out was to figure out how the paths linked up because I knew that's where the banjo player would be, and where the woman had gone to listen.

I was running, but I didn't know from what. I could barely see the sky above. I thought the fragrance I was inhaling was honeysuckle. Then I smashed headfirst into Handsome John and sent him reeling back and bleeding.

"Don't you know where you're going?" I screamed.

He started running away from me.

"I thought you did," he said, wiping blood from his face.

I tried to help him, but he was dizzy from the collision and fell back down himself.

"You lost, too, ain't you? You don' even know which side you're on."

Blood was spurting from his eye socket, like Oedipus.

"No. No, I'm not. I know where I am," I told him, protesting too much. "I'm doing research."

Then I stopped arguing and listened. The sound of the banjo was intense, very close. I saw the banjo player – first his bare feet, then the rest of him – all except for his face, which wouldn't come clear. The woman standing there, in the spell

*of his banjo, was Una Vida. Just as he realized it wasn't hon-
eysuckle at all but Shalimar, she turned her head toward me –
but it was my mother's face.*

"So you weren't bathed in sweat after all," Elvira said quietly. "Those were tears on your face when you woke up."

Cruz nodded.

Elvira's interpretation startled Cruz at first; then he realized it made sense: The banjo player was a child – that's
why his feet were bare.

"Una Vida had a child," Elvira said. "Find that child and
we'll help her find herself."

"My mother had a child, too," Cruz said.

Elvira's eyes were shining.

"I don't even know her real name."

"The universe knows her name," Elvira said. "Stay open
to its signs. It's been hammering down your doors."

While they were waiting for their second cup of coffee,
Cruz told Elvira he'd be right back. He ran across the street
to find Handsome John in the carriage line. He needed to
ask him what he knew about Una Vida.

"Looking for someone?" one of the other drivers asked
after Cruz had searched the line of carriages twice.

The disappointment on his face must have been obvious.

"I guess Handsome John is out on a ride?" he asked.

The driver looked at him. "Only the ride across Jordan,"
he finally said.

Cruz turned to face the man. "What?"

"Handsome John died."

"He died? What are you talking about? We just took a
ride with him around midnight!"

"Then that was his last fare. Ole Red pulled up to the

Square with him still in his seat. But he was down and out for the count. Still clutching his whip."

"I don't believe it." Cruz was stunned.

"See that stack of flyers over there?" The driver pointed to a small metal table near the entrance to the plaza. "Take a look for yourself."

Cruz sleepwalked to the little table and picked up one of the flyers. Things happened fast in the Quarter. His eyes widened as he read the words, as if it was all an elaborate practical joke – or as if he were still dreaming:

**You are cordially invited
To the jazz funeral of John H. Richards
"Handsome John"
Sunday, October 27th at 6:00 P.M.
A.M.E. Church, downtown**

Sunday was the day after tomorrow, the day before Cruz was to leave for Madrid. Though he'd known Handsome John only a few hours, having him appear so prominently in his dream, Cruz's disbelief gave way to an inexplicable sense of loss. He walked in a daze back to Café du Monde. Elvira looked at his hand and saw the flyer.

"What's that?"

*

Elvira and Cruz made their way to the river, just wanting to sit down for a minute. The flyer was still clenched in Cruz's fist. A streetcar was loading in front of them, so they stopped on the street side of the tracks.

"I wonder if Red will know the difference," Cruz finally said lamely as a mother and her two children boarded the car awkwardly with a double stroller and an array of baby accessories.

"I imagine she will," said Elvira.

The streetcar moved down the line. Soon enough, so did its rumble.

"Taking us to the Cornstalk Inn was somehow destined to be his last task in life," Cruz said.

Elvira nodded. "I'm sure of it."

*

The next day was a blur for Cruz, between catching up from his truancy and making sure he was prepared for the trip to Madrid. Though it was rare, he asked Zevie to come in on a Saturday to help him get organized. He felt a little guilty. *She* hadn't taken nearly two days off in the middle of the week.

Just before three, the time Cruz had told her she could knock off, Zevie walked into his office with a package and handed it to him.

"You might want to save room for this," she said. His raised eyebrow was all she needed to continue. "There's no return address."

Cruz took the package and examined it. He could make out "Jessica" but not the last name.

"Can you trace it with the carrier?"

Zevie frowned. "It was hand-delivered to reception." Before he could ask the question, she said, "I already checked with them. They *did* make her sign in, though there's a note that she had no ID. The signature was nearly illegible, but it looks like 'Jessica Marshall.'"

Cruz frowned. The woman who wrote the calligraphy he'd seen in the garden had handwriting anything but illegible – unless the illegibility on the package was intentional. By that time he had opened it and again recognized the calligraphy in the words written on the same pink paper: "Una Vida's drawings." Jessica was offering them to him for his appraisal, as if she knew he'd find in them what she needed him to find. Though he was tempted, there was simply no time. He rewrapped the drawings and tucked them into his briefcase to examine on the plane.

*

Cruz was exhausted by the time Sunday afternoon rolled around. He'd stayed up most of the night catching up and leaving instructions for his research team. Though he'd be away only five days, so many things were going on that it might as well be a month. He was aware he might be overestimating the need for his input, but the awareness didn't stop him from making sure every one of his staff had a handwritten note urging them toward achievement. Maintaining the pressure was part of his responsibility, he judged; great discoveries were made under pressure.

But he'd really overextended himself Saturday night because he wanted to attend Handsome John's funeral, which would take two precious hours out of his final day in town. He wasn't about to miss it. Attending was the least he and Elvira could do for the man who'd spent the last hours of his life guiding them through the labyrinth of the Quarter, the labyrinth of jazz, the maze of Una Vida's world – and into the heart of the labyrinth he had dedicated his life to exploring.

A jazz band was leading the carriage bearing John's coffin into the cemetery, slow-playing the traditional "When the Saints Go Marching In" as Cruz parked on the periphery and inserted himself discreetly among the mourners. For a man who was "only a driver," Handsome John enjoyed an impressive following on his last ride. Elvira estimated at least three hundred people.

The woman standing next to them at the graveside saw his eyes move among the crowd. Her hair was a deep gray color and hung down her back in a long braid tied with thick leather cordage. Her neck was adorned with amber and her ears with turquoise. She was thin, but not too much so. Her eyes were deep brown, almost black.

"Over 300," she said, as if she'd just performed the same calculation.

She allowed her face to open up into a full smile, as if she'd caught him stealing cookies. Cruz smiled back.

"He must have been a wonderful man."

She smiled back at him. "Nobody could be like Handsome John. He took people where they needed to go, but only left them off there if they knew where they were." Before Cruz could process the statement, the woman added, "You must be Dr. Cruz. And this is your wife?"

Cruz was startled, but moved his hand to shake hers. Elvira smiled and did the same.

"I'm Amitė Deerkill," she said.

"Amitė, the tarot reader?"

The woman nodded. "So we both know surprising things. But I don't have to read cards to tell you you're about to take a journey."

"Are my pre-travel jitters that obvious?" Cruz laughed, drawing the attention of the other mourners.

Amitė's withering look turned their eyes away.

"I'm not talking about that trip," she went on. "I'm talking about the trip that you and the rabbit will take, which will heal you both – the journey that isn't just *your* journey."

Cruz's eyes met his wife's. She remembered what he'd told her about the woman like a rabbit that Stompleg had warned him against.

After the brief graveside ceremony, the Cruzes allowed her to lead them to a shaded table where she insisted on reading Alvaro's cards.

"I know you're in a hurry," she said, "but the time it'll take will come back to you when you need it."

Elvira urged him to go along with a nod.

The cards Amitė pulled from her pocket weren't the traditional tarots. Seeing Cruz's glance, she explained that she used her own cards, based on pictures her father had drawn for her as a child. The images were of a Cherokee mythology that added up to form the metaphysical basis for reality as it is seen by the living – as well as the unseen spirit world out on its borderland.

Cruz watched Amitė arrange the table with a flat piece of deerskin that she'd unfolded carefully, on which she placed three eagle feathers, a handful of porcupine quills and the tooth of a grizzly. Once the deck of worn homemade cards was in front of her, she asked Cruz to cut them. Amitė then spread the cards across the deerskin. She took Cruz's right hand in her own and with a single whip-like gesture, removed all the tension from it. Then she instructed him to place his hand on the card he'd been guided to place it on. Without reflecting, Cruz did as he was instructed. His hand came to rest on the ninth card from the end on the left side of the table. Amitė asked him to hand her the face-down card, and Cruz did.

"You know what card is in my hand?" Amitė asked, without taking her eyes off him.

"I have no idea."

"You don't need ideas when the truth is self-evident. Don't tell me your idea, tell me what you know," Amitė insisted.

"I don't know what I know," Cruz stumbled.

"You don't know what your dreams mean, but you see them plain as day, don't you? Tell me how a dream is different from waking life."

Cruz didn't answer, though his brain was sending insistent signals of cornfields to him. Elvira watched, warning him with her glance not to break his concentration. Amitė turned over the card.

"There is no difference," she said.

The picture on the card was one she called the *Corn Maiden*. Cruz stared at the card and then looked up to find Amitė and Elvira staring at him.

"The Corn Maiden is the youthful female deity parallel to the Blue God and is sometimes a trickster. But don't mistake her childlike form for a lack of power. She's an aspect of the Star Goddess and partakes of everything that she is. She brought you together with the rabbit for the sake of a journey. This journey is for life itself. It is bigger than you. You two are only the messengers, and you need each other to penetrate the mystery that burdens you both. Your two hands must act as one if this deed that must be done is to set things right."

Amitė Deerkill spoke no more, and, though Cruz offered, would not accept money for the reading.

"This is for John," she said.

"Can I ask one question?" Cruz said.

"You can ask. But I may not be the one to answer it."

"Why me?"

"Because you have a big brain, and a strong heart. And a deep soul."

Amitė's face opened up again, and the smile Elvira gave him lasted all the way to Madrid.

Chapter 7

Showered and dressed, garment bag in hand, Cruz leaned over to kiss Elvira. Her gentleness permeated him as she held him close for a minute.

"Got everything?" she asked. "Billfold, passport – "

"I have everything I need right here," he said, touching her chin. "Are you sure I shouldn't stay?"

"It's not the same, dear," she said. "You're needed there. That's your job. Whatever is happening here can wait." She smiled and kissed him again, on the cheek this time. "Stay away from rabbits till you get back."

Their laughter rang together as though synchronized.

A piece of toast with blackberry jam later, a shot of orange juice, and Cruz was out the door to meet the blue cab posted outside.

In the security line at Louis Armstrong International, Cruz pulled out his laptop as instructed and placed it in the gray plastic bin. When he opened his work bag, he caught a glimpse of the pictures drawn by Una Vida's hand. Something about one of the images startled him as a security woman rushed him to put his bag on the belt.

Cruz couldn't get the horrifying image out of his mind. It resembled a Francisco Goya he had first seen as a teenager paging through an art book of his aunt's – a disturbing piece posthumously titled *Saturn Devouring his Son*. It was a painting of a monster-sized man holding up a small human carcass with both hands. The head had already been eaten and the body lay limp in the giant's hands with thick red blood spurting down. One arm was already gone; the other was being gnawed on and was bloodied. The giant's hand covered the boy's back; the eyes were pure wolf.

On the plane, Cruz reexamined the drawing and scanned the others. The devouring image was placed back in the manila envelope marked in calligraphy, "Most Recent." He focused on the early portraits – safe and pastoral. Those realistic pictures drawn by Una Vida also resembled the early Goya – the court painter given to pleasing his patrons and offering them honor, not interpretation. A steady hand and mind had drawn them. The contradiction between that and the confused scrawl on the back was remarkable. One looked as if it had been painted by a virtuoso, the other by a child of six.

Cruz realized that losing one life, *una vida*, was equivalent to losing an entire ecosystem – to losing a piece of history and a link in the chain that connected us all. Before a mind dies, it should be explored as fully as possible. One mind could save the species, alert us to something we all desperately needed to know.

Somehow, Una Vida's brain had learned how to use art to combat the disease that was trying to shut it down before its mission was complete.

*

Cruz's flight arrived in Madrid forty minutes late. Between a delayed takeoff and the long transatlantic flight, Cruz landed numb and exhausted. By the time his taxi arrived at the Hotel Villa Magna, not too far from El Prado, it was after 4:00 A.M. in Spain – though it was only 8:00 P.M. back home. He would force himself to sleep. He knew if he didn't, he'd have a rough time the next day.

The Victorian tiles in the bathroom floor felt cold on his bare feet as he ran the hot water and breathed in the steam. After five minutes in the too-small porcelain tub, he began to relax. The towels were slightly thinner than what he was used to in the States, so he used two, slightly warmed, to cover his eyes and chest while he meditated to clear his mind.

With his black mask over his eyes to keep out the morning light, he sank into the large bed and drifted off. He woke hours later, not remembering a single dream.

Refreshed for what felt like the first time in days, he saw that his cell phone was turned off.

"I must've really been tired," he thought.

He picked up the hotel phone for room service and ordered melon and fresh *Manchego* cheese. Cruz's Argentinean palate preferred Spanish cheese to all others, so he ate as much as he could when he came to Madrid. After he had washed and dressed and consumed the modest portion typically served in Europe, he checked the messages on his cell phone.

His friend and host from the Universidad de Alcala, Ricardo Palacios-Pelaez, had called twice. He and Cruz had planned to meet for a late lunch before the formal meeting at the University's Madrid center. Ricardo and Cruz held patents together and were meeting to discuss how those chemicals had done as they went through Phase I clinical trials, a process Ricardo had come to New Orleans a few weeks earlier to initiate. They were both grateful to their universities for allowing them to collaborate on drug discovery and excited to take things directly from the lab bench to the bedside where they could see their research actually affect patients' lives. Someday soon they hoped to do that for Alzheimer's.

Cruz made his way to the Cafe *Islas Cies,* a new place that had opened since his last trip to Madrid. When he got there, Ricardo was already waiting with his neuroscientist wife, Chus, a bright medicinal chemist from the Universidad de Alcala, Julio Alvarez-Builla, and Carlos Sunkel. Cruz was greeted with hugs and kisses all around and flooded with salutations in his native tongue. His friends hadn't ordered yet, but had begun a serious attack on a carafe of *vino tinto.* Cruz loved that about Spain; the patience of the place. In most U.S. cities he visited, lunch was strictly business – it seemed that more and more things were. Sometimes it felt as if every minute was judged as time either wasted or well-spent. Anything else left you with a sense of guilt.

But, like New Orleans, Spain was totally different. To talk art, religion, politics, and wine with fellow researchers and scientists was the norm, not the exception. To laugh loudly, to hug, to catch up on family and friends, to share something that couldn't be described in any other way but as friendship, was the joy of being in Spain – as it had been in his native Argentina in the old days before the *Guerra Sucia.* Collaborating with Ricardo's group was a sheer delight for him.

As Cruz sat down and opened the menu, Ricardo reached for the carafe and filled his glass with *Marques de Arienzo Crianza* from *Rioja.* Chus passed him a small morsel of *jamon pata negra* – the finest ham in Spain, from the native black-hoofed Iberian pig raised on a steady diet of acorns. The taste was nutty, aged, and smooth – truly worthy of savoring. The taste of the *jamon* brought the wine alive, and Cruz began to feel the pulse of his native culture.

As they nibbled on *jamon and cabrales,* a pungent cave-aged blue cheese from the rugged Picos de Europa Mountains of Asturias, the conversation began to flow. The subject turned to the currently debated controversy surrounding the Black Paintings of Francisco Goya. It became startlingly clear to Cruz immediately that his friends had been talking about Goya while they awaited his arrival.

"Oddly enough," he told them, "I was thinking about Goya on the plane here."

He told them a little about his encounter with Una Vida, but didn't mention her drawings. His Spanish friends knew that Cruz had always been particularly fascinated by the brains of artists, convinced that it found ways of dealing with reality that most people, whose lives were focused on the rational and practical, rarely explored.

As the waiter came to clear this first course, Julio smiled.

"We have a surprise for you, Alvaro," he beamed.

The head waiter made an almost-ceremonial entrance with five plates of *Angulas a la bilbaina* – baby eels in oil and garlic sauce – balanced on his arms. Exorbitantly-priced, that European eel was renowned for its strength and sacrifice as much as for its taste of tender sublimity. The tiny eels made a five-month journey across the Atlantic from Europe to spawn in the Sargasso Sea, a seaweed-covered body of water between Bermuda and Puerto Rico. The European eels co-mingled with their American cousins, deposited vast quantities of eggs, and then died. It was up to their offspring to make the harrowing 4,000-mile return trip. Born transparent and no more than a quarter-inch long, the tiny eels latched onto the Gulf Stream and surfed their way to Europe, growing to nearly three inches by the time they arrived, a journey that took three years. You barely needed to cook them: a bit of olive oil, garlic, the smallest amount of crushed chile pepper, just a minute over a flame, and right into your mouth. They were served extremely hot and rushed to your table. You ate them with a wooden fork crafted for just that purpose.

The group devoured their eels in silence, a gourmet's communion. When they had done justice to the eels, Ricardo, Julio, Carlos and Chus pronounced the whole contemporary controversy over Goya's Black Paintings nothing more than an art historian's tempest in a teapot. Chus was convinced that Goya had in fact not painted those last paintings himself, as some scholars suggested. Her theory was that his thirty-year-old mistress, Leocadia Weiss, had painted them as a kind of homage to the great master, trying to both copy and interpret him simultaneously.

When Chus asked Cruz if he agreed, he patted his lips with his napkin. He didn't want to offend her, didn't want to spoil the lunch. He'd been content to have the four of them rapt together in awe of the mastery of Francisco de Goya. It was as if the deeply disturbing drawings he'd examined on the plane had stalked him.

Before his friends could put Cruz on the spot, the main course arrived, the gastronomic climax toward which the tapas had been building like a crescendo. It was *rabo de toro,* a dish Cruz had not tasted for some time. The juniper berries, the attendant head waiter explained, were from the woods of *Aragon*; the recipe came to the owner of the new restaurant from his great grandfather, who'd grown up in Andalucia, a region famous for its oxtail stew cooked with carrot, onion, salt, paprika, peppercorns, tomato, thyme, oregano, a bit of white wine. The key was the meat, though, its quality and the length of time it was cooked – slowly, for a minimum of three hours.

After that sumptuous feast, there was room for nothing else, save a bit of fire – a small glass of Pacharan, a sloe berry-based digestif from the Basque region that had originated in medieval times. Then Chus put the pressure on Cruz.

"Answer my question," she said.

"It's been a while since I've seen those paintings. Why don't we go over to the Prado and take a look?"

Julio laughed. "Always the scientist, Cruz. Don't give an opinion before you view the empirical evidence again, is that it?"

"Is there anything wrong with being a scientist?" Cruz quipped.

"Empiricism is one thing," Chus said, "but the veil of objectivity can't shield you from telling the truth. After you view them again, you'll still have to make a judgment."

"And I will," Cruz replied. "But first, I must see them again."

Julio had to beg off to further prepare for the next day's meeting. But Ricardo, Chus, and Carlos joined Cruz.

The Black Paintings had been created at Goya's *Quinta del Sordo*, so named for the man who had lived in the modest country abode before Goya and who was also deaf, as Goya would become at the age of forty-six. At the age of seventy-two, Goya lived with his mistress as a self-exiled recluse after having served royalty for years through his art. He felt embittered about the world and became lost in a shrine of his own making. In that simple rectangular house, he was safe from the judgments of Restoration-era Madrid over his relationship with a much younger woman. The only voices he heard were those that spoke within him. He lived in memory, unaware of the rhythms and tones that howled just outside his door. There in the country, buried in the caverns of his mind and uninterrupted by outside demands, Goya created what scholars and critics would later dub the Black Paintings.

The fourteen haunting masterpieces were untitled and unadorned. The artist didn't even use canvases to paint them; he painted them right on the walls. To get them into the Prado, the entire *Quinta del Sordo* had to be dismantled. Painted in oils, directly onto the plaster, they remained some of the most disturbing images in all of modern art. Goya didn't title them, probably never intended to show them to the outside world. The images reflected his inner mythology, a self-referencing abyss painstakingly depicted – as if to help him remember the hell of his deteriorating self-awareness, even if he should one day be redeemed to heaven.

Maybe it was the wine and the *angulas,* maybe it was just meant to be, but as Cruz looked upon *Saturn Devouring His Son*, and next to it a painting of a man of eighty or so with a long white flowing beard, walking with a cane – he suddenly understood the connection. He understood what Una Vida and Goya had in common: Both were artists, who'd built a lifetime career out of surfing freely among the oceans of possibilities; who had defied the inhibitions selected by others as a safer route to personality.

Believing that our lives are individuated independent entities is one of the biggest illusions humans like to perpetuate. Especially in a society that values individuality above all else, to think otherwise could border on treason. But the way our minds were born – through evolution, personal genetics, and the power of our environment over us – we were never alone. Our families lived on in us, along with a common universal history of survival through adaptation. There was nothing inherently mystical or religious about those facts, though someone could certainly read them that way. In the tortured drawings of Una Vida, as in the black paintings of Goya, the artist's brain was expressing its awareness of the breakdown of the grand illusion. Cruz knew nothing certain of Goya's pathology, but there on the solemn walls of the Prado, bearing the darkly colorful passions of that great artist, Cruz could see an imagination terrified by its own demise. For both of them – Una Vida with her music and Goya with those paintings – art itself had become the last and only hope. Cruz thought of his own intense work at the lab and how it reminded him daily of the statement by another great and tortured Spanish artist, Salvador Dali: "The difference between myself and a madman is that I am not mad."

In the painting that attracted Cruz's attention, if he looked only at the old man, the picture wasn't the least bit disturbing. But right alongside him, whispering in his ear, was a shadow-self, a demon of such terror that most felt their innards shake as their optic nerves slowly registered its presence. Confronted with the image in the past, Cruz's interpretation had been that the creature was simply whispering to the old man; but at that moment, in that light, and in light of his experiences with Una Vida's Alzheimer's, the wide-mouthed demon looked as if he was poised to devour the unsuspecting man's ear – preparatory to swallowing his entire brain.

Cruz felt tightness in his chest. The creature seemed to be looking at him as much as he was looking at it. It wouldn't let go. What was the demon saying to the old man? Though repulsed, Cruz was drawn closer. He wanted to listen in on the conversation between the old man and his demon. But as he listened in his imagination, he realized the demon's voice was his own. It was the voice that had been torment-ing him since his mother's death, the voice that was telling him he could never forgive himself.

Cruz thought he had only shouted it to himself, but his friends turned when they heard him scream at the painting, "*Porque?* Why?" as if he could erase the image from the world. But Goya would not allow it. Cruz's heart began to race; his back was wet with perspiration.

His friends left the paintings they were studying and rushed over to him. Tears were burning in the corners of his eyes as he collapsed to his knees.

"What's wrong, Cruz? All the color's gone from your face," he heard Chus say as if she were talking to a stranger. He couldn't answer at first.

Finally, he managed the word, "*Agua.*"

She fetched water in a paper cup and Cruz drank it down quickly. They removed his jacket, got him up off the floor, and onto a bench.

He didn't tell them about Jessica or Stompleg. He didn't tell them anything further. He simply drank the water and as they all marveled over the power of those paintings, felt the immense burden on his shoulders of all the pain and suffering humans had experienced from the beginning of time. He could see clearly what he had failed to see before: *una vida*, one life made all the difference; each life was as important as all life. His lifelong mission of unraveling the secrets of the brain to alleviate the suffering of those whose brains had been disarrayed by disease was now clearly yoked with exploring Una Vida's personal loss and anguish with his last ounce of strength.

"Goya did these, all right," Cruz finally said, strength and confidence returning to his voice. "There's no way a thirty-year-old could have done them. These were painted by a master, a tortured master crying out."

Even Chus was convinced. "The power of empiricism," she said. "The reality of momentary experience tells a truth that no memory could rival." She had been won over by Cruz's reaction.

"Nothing could explain this power, unless it was that

Goya's memories were actually happening in the present moment," Cruz whispered to himself between sips of water.

*

At dinner that night, which didn't come until 10:00 P.M., they all joked about what had happened in the museum. Cruz's antics were recounted to Julio as if Charlie Chaplin had been there in his place. Ricardo laughed until tears rolled down his eyes as he reported Chus being won over by the dramatic reaction.

"Cruz always did love the theatre," goaded Carlos. "The use of spectacle to win over an audience has never been lost on him – a fine application of Aristotle's *Poetics*."

Chus frowned, ignoring Carlos' inside joke.

"He had me fooled. I can't believe he's that good an actor."

They stayed off the *grappa* and kept the subject of art off the table, and though there was lots of laughter and light-hearted talk, Cruz felt as if the group that had seen him on his knees today was a bit different tonight.

"Irrational loose ends," as Ricardo called them, made him particularly uncomfortable, but to Chus, as to Elvira, they marked the beginning of wisdom. Chus stole glances at Cruz to see if something in him had been changed. What he'd experienced, in her mind, was a conversion.

Chapter 8

*A*fter the agreements between the two universities had been initialed by both sides, Cruz settled in for the long plane ride home. The United States and Spain were so different; it made him feel fortunate to be landing in New Orleans, Louisiana – easily the most "Spain-like" city in the U.S. Despite its "French" reputation, the Cabildo, next to St. Louis Cathedral, was enough to prove New Orleans' Spanish birthright. Near the end of the French and Indian War in 1762, France was about to lose all of Louisiana to the British. To avoid having to give up the "Isle of Orleans," they made a secret treaty with Spain called the "Treaty of Fontainebleau," in which the isle was ceded to Spain. With the 1763 Treaty of Paris that ended that war, Great Britain gained control of all of Louisiana except New Orleans, which was still under Spanish control. Led by a Spanish governor, much like Cruz's own native Argentina once had been, the city took on a Spanish flavor.

The Cabildo had been named for the Spanish council

that met there. It eventually became a museum famous for being the place where the Louisiana Purchase was ratified and where Napoleon's death mask was housed. Yet another major legacy from the Spanish was the Pontalba Apartments, the oldest apartments in the country, a mirror-image pair of red brick architectural masterpieces that flanked either side of Jackson Square. To the right was the Lower Pontalba, owned by the State of Louisiana; and to the left, the Upper Pontalba, owned by the City of New Orleans. The apartments had originally been built by the Baroness Micaela Pontalba in the 1840s. She was the daughter of a wealthy Spaniard, Don Almonester y Rojas, and she inherited the land around the square from him. She wanted to leave a classic European mark on the city of New Orleans; those apartments were her contribution.

Exiled Acadians were welcomed by the Spanish city of New Orleans and agriculture thrived – sugarcane and rice did well under the guidance of Spanish farmers. After Spain declared war on Great Britain in 1779, New Orleans became a port of great assistance to the thirteen colonies engaged in fighting the American Revolutionary War. New Orleans provided supplies and moral support to the new burgeoning America.

Also during Spanish rule, the only "free people of color" in the country lived in New Orleans. They were called Creoles and were of French or West Indian descent. Property records of 1803 in New Orleans show that more than one quarter of the houses and estates on the main roads and thoroughfares were owned by free people of color and that the majority were households headed by single women with a litter of children.

Cruz never failed to be impressed by the aerial view of his adopted city – lakes and rivers and bayous and canals expanding in a kaleidoscope of colors and a labyrinth of water and flora. He'd read that the Port of New Orleans was the largest in the world, with 13,000 miles of waterways. In 1800, New Orleans had returned to the possession of the French, and Spanish rule was gone – but not forgotten. Thomas Jefferson feared that Napoleon would hold on to New Orleans and make it a stronghold of American resistance. But when Jefferson finally got up the gumption to approach him about the matter in 1803, Napoleon had already decided to sell Jefferson the lot, and the Louisiana Purchase became history.

The name of the family of Spanish viceroys that ruled New Orleans from 1762 through 1800 was "Bourbon." They probably wouldn't appreciate the irony of their name coming to be singularly associated with the "French Quarter" of the city or with the most notorious of that Quarter's intoxicated nightlife, but history was a dowager who took her own route.

Cruz's New Orleans had become a grand jambalaya of Indian, French, Spanish, Italian, African, Creole, Irish – and God knew how many other influences. A New Orleans seafood gumbo had hints of good Spanish *paella*. Such things were not coincidence, but a syncretistic mashing together of cultures. New Orleans was a brain all its own, having shaped the personality it showed to the world, and the infinite secret personalities that came to the surface only in encounters with its Una Vidas, from everything it had inherited and experienced through the centuries.

Cruz, too, had been thrown into the city's jambalaya, an Argentine by birth turned American who had been born in a place once ruled by Spain and later immigrated to a place once ruled by Spain. He was coming to believe that his peculiar destiny was unique, though. In some way, he would play a part in the final stages of Una Vida's life – if only he could understand the signs that were being laid out for him.

＊

Stompleg looked relieved to see him, recognizing Cruz immediately when Cruz waved from the shallow staircase leading up the levee. His banjo sounded livelier than usual, Cruz thought. Elvira smiled at the merry sound echoing along the river.

"Where's Una Vida today?" Cruz asked the musician.

Stompleg stopped strumming to answer him.

"Takin' a walk by the river," he said. "Found somebody who remembered her from a long time ago."

At Cruz's look of excitement, Stompleg hurried to add, "But I need to talk to you first." He doffed his hat to Elvira. "This must be the missus."

Cruz introduced them and Elvira told Stompleg she loved the sound of his playing. Stompleg's voice took on a conspiratorial tone, as he moved closer to Cruz's face.

"I got accepted," he said.

"Accepted?"

Stompleg nodded, a mixture of pride and guilt crossing his face. "The Music Maker Foundation."

Cruz remembered that Stompleg had gone for an interview at some foundation. Now the name rang a bell. The North Carolina foundation housed street artists who met certain criteria of performance and provided them, for the rest of their lives, with a safe residence and facilities for continuing to perform their arts – even to make recordings – in a supportive and respectful environment. Parker would later tell Cruz that the foundation's advisory board included the likes of B.B. King, Bonnie Raitt, Dickey Betts, Jimmy Herring, and Tom Rankin, who maintained vigilant watch over the purity of the foundation's operations.

"They're gonna take me back to Durham. I passed the test!" A tear appeared in Stompleg's eyes. "First thing I done good in twenty years," he said. "Probably record a CD after that, then go on tour with other Music Maker artists. They're gonna set me up for life."

Now the tears were unrestrained and Cruz put his arm around the man's shoulder.

"You deserve it," Cruz said. "Sometimes Fortune remembers her children."

"Who would've believed that someone like me could get a fresh start at the age of sixty-one, and finally get to put my music out in the world the way it's supposed to be…I told you the blues saved my life." Stompleg wiped his eyes with his frayed sleeve.

"Does Una Vida know?"

"I tried to tell her, but she just heard it as a part of some fantasy in her mind. She don't have no idea what it mean for her. That's why I'm glad to see you," Stompleg said. "I don't know what to do."

Cruz and Elvira exchanged glances. Stompleg was pulling out a thick wad of green from his pocket.

"There's $320.00 dollars here. It's all hers. I set aside half every time she played with me. The rent's paid at my studio until the end of the month. I let her stay there the last little while. If she wants to keep it after that, it's $275.00 plus utilities. Landlord's a real good guy, loves the blues. She can mostly take care of herself – " He looked away.

"Did you tell the relief organization about her?" Elvira asked.

"Haven't seen her much since I got back." Stompleg evaded Elvira's question. "I think she's mad at me for leaving. She showed up down here today and hardly spoke to me. Besides, I figure Jessica probably wants to take care of her now."

Stompleg wasn't looking into Cruz's eyes as he spoke, forcing his voice to the matter-of-factness of an accountant discussing a tax return.

"Where is Jessica? What's she have to do with Una Vida? I thought you told me – " Cruz pressed, trying to break through the businesslike demeanor Stompleg had assumed.

Stompleg interrupted him. "I know what I said, but people say a lot of things. I'm sure Jessica's all right now. I was probably just being paranoid."

Stompleg had packed up his banjo and now sat perched on his little stool, rolling a cigarette.

"Have you seen her?" Cruz asked. "She sent me some of Una Vida's drawings."

Stompleg looked mystified by the information.

"I tried calling her all day today, and for the last two days – but got no answer." His face turned serious. "Last time that happened, she overdosed." Stompleg shrugged. "She's a druggie. That's what they do when they can't handle stuff. So far, she's come out of it okay."

"She's lucky. One too many overdoses and she's done for," Cruz commented.

Elvira looked concerned. The tension between the two men was palpable and she didn't understand it. Some macho exchange had just taken place. For the life of her, she had no idea what it was about.

"Well, something brought you here just now," Stompleg continued. "You're the doctor. You know about these things. I don't know nothin' 'cept it's time to save myself befo' it's too late. Too long in Angola and too long on the junk before that, I ain't never had a chance. I want what's best for Una Vida, and I sure as hell know I ain't got what it takes to care for her. It's a shame when a woman as old and as talented as her has to share a 350-square-foot studio apartment with an ex-con." Stompleg looked at Elvira as he spoke.

"Sounds like you've been a good friend to her. I'd say she's had a lot more than that since she met you," Elvira smiled. "Why don't you keep that money for your travels?" she added softly.

"I couldn't do that. You take it for her," Stompleg said, pressing the green roll into Cruz's left hand without meeting his eyes. "She gets a little anxious around sundown... Listen for me on the radio," he called back as Cruz and Elvira watched him disappear across the tracks and into the Quarter, his grocery cart of music dragging on old wheels behind him.

"I know what you're thinking, Alvaro," Elvira said. "But there's no way an organization like that would take on someone with Alzheimer's."

"I'm sure you're right."

"You can't blame him, you know," Elvira went on. "He did more than most. Sounds like he found just what he needed, and not a moment too soon."

They sat holding hands with the silent river as witness, and when Cruz looked up, Una Vida wasn't far off – as if the mist had cleared to reveal her. Cruz pointed her out to Elvira and the two of them made their way down the river walk toward her.

Cruz thought about Una Vida coming to New Orleans in 1933. By then, most of the great jazz had already hit the road for Harlem and Chicago. In that year, Duke Ellington and Louis Armstrong were both on tour in Europe, Prohibition was gone and lots of the speakeasies were going out of business. Storyville was a thing of the past. Ellington was famous in America, but still unwelcome in many hotels and restaurants in the towns where he played. As a way of dealing with the embedded bigotry, Ellington and his band got their own Pullman car, where they slept and dined throughout their American tour. Duke usually went straight from the train yard to the concert hall and back again in those years. His fans would come down to the yard to see him and say he traveled like the president. Duke always came out to greet his fans with a smile.

Armstrong was the star of Europe that year, famous for blowing a particular high-pitched note on the trumpet that no other player could reproduce. The tone made a rough callous in the center of Armstrong's upper lip, which was prone to infection. His manager at the time booked him several nights in a row, refusing to let him rest, wanting to make as much money from him as possible. One night in London, Armstrong's upper lip split apart right on stage during a high note. Blood spurted everywhere. He went into semi-retirement for eight months, returning to the States more than a year after he'd left. When he got back home, the Great Satchmo had trouble finding steady work.

Charlie Parker was thirteen at that time, learning to play the baritone horn in Kansas City, Missouri, by imitating the old-time jazz musicians.

Cruz marveled at all the greats playing in those speakeasies. Una Vida had to be one story in ten thousand, but one every bit as worth discovering and telling for posterity. How she had gotten by in those years, especially if she had a child at that time, was a testament to the strength of her will. The fact that she'd survived those years at all and was still surviving and walking around should count for something in the grand scheme of things, Cruz thought. The recesses of Una Vida's synaptic connections held more songs than he and Elvira could possibly imagine, which accounted for the feeling of sacredness he felt in her presence.

The woman now speaking to Una Vida was well dressed and spoke in a French accent – but not Louisiana French. They watched the woman pat Una Vida's back, walk away, and bring a handkerchief to her face as she sat down on one of the green curved benches facing the Mississippi.

*

Cruz went over to the woman on the bench and sat down beside her. When she'd stopped her tears, he introduced himself and quickly told her how he'd come to know Una Vida, wanted to help her, and needed to find out anything he could about her. The French woman, who introduced herself as Mezille, told Cruz that she and her first husband – many years her senior, she added – had first seen Una Vida sing and play jazz in Paris years ago, and that they'd made a habit of coming back to New Orleans for years to visit her husband's sister; when they did, they always tried to catch Una Vida in a jazz club.

"Such a talented singer and painter," Mezille said. "It's unbearably sad what's happening to her."

She added that she hadn't been back to New Orleans since her first husband's sister had died ten years earlier.

"I know what she's got," Mezille said. "I recognize all the signs. My third husband, God rest his soul, got Alzheimer's at the age of fifty-eight." Mezille changed her tone. "My first husband named her Una Vida, you know. He was a Spaniard of tremendous exuberance. When he first saw her perform, long before he met me, he was captivated by her and insisted on waiting by the stage door to meet her after the show. She finally came out, looking even taller and more beautiful up close than she did on stage. My husband grabbed her and kissed both her cheeks and said, 'You are life itself, you are Una Vida.'

"From then on, she listed her name in all the programs simply as Una Vida."

"Did you know her real name before?" Cruz asked.

"If I did, I have long since forgotten. To me, she was, and always will be, only Una Vida."

Cruz noticed that Una Vida was staring out at the river and opening and closing her clarinet case so it made a clicking sound. Elvira was caressing the instrument with her fingers and they were talking about it. He saw that his wife had worked her magic. The two women had bonded, as though they were lifelong friends.

"When the disease first came, we were still able to go out and do things together," Mezille continued. "An exhibition of Goya was being shown at the Louvre, on loan from El Prado. I didn't know what the Black Paintings were, but I thought it would be an interesting way to spend the day. Do you know Goya's works?"

Restraining a burst of laughter that Cruz knew she could only take as inappropriate, he merely nodded, feeling a pulse come alive in his stomach and beat out a rhythm that threatened to knock him off his feet – bringing him right back to Spain and the paintings, and his involuntary acquaintance with the floor of the museum. Although he heard the words Mezille was saying, Cruz was experiencing the most intense moment of déjà vu he'd ever felt.

"He pointed one of the dark images out to me that to this day I wish I'd never seen because it's now become a permanent fixture of my dreams. This picture was of a kindly bearded old man that looked the way you might imagine Moses. And you looked at this old man and felt fine, but then you saw this horrible demon beside him like an alter ego that was poised to attack him.

"I remember feeling a sense of horror when I heard my husband's voice, 'I'm at war with myself,' he said. 'And the man you are familiar with is losing that war. When it's done, the wretched creature still standing will be unknown to us both.' Goya knew something of this, and I hate him for it. When I asked my husband about that episode later, he'd forgotten all of it; didn't even remember seeing that painting or being at the Louvre."

Mezille had let her handkerchief go and taken Cruz's hand with force.

"I understand better than anyone else could possibly understand," Cruz said.

"I came back to New Orleans to forget, but finding Una Vida made me remember. Is there no place on earth where this disease will not follow me?"

She dropped Cruz's hand as if it were a bad omen and walked away.

*

There'd been no discussion. Neither of them had even considered an alternative. They simply brought Una Vida home with them. Elvira held her by the hand until they got to Cruz's car, both of them giggling like long-lost school chums.

The bump at the entrance to his driveway startled Una Vida and brought Cruz back from his cogitations to the moment at hand. Una Vida looked at Cruz, but nothing registered.

"Where you taking me?"

Cruz didn't want to lie to her, but how could he explain anything? He didn't know the whole plan himself yet. All he knew was that he wanted to get her into Malta Park as quickly as possible for the round-the-clock care she needed.

"We've brought you home," Elvira said.

Una Vida looked straight at Cruz, recognition dawning in her eyes.

"I knew you was gonna come around. Ain't a man gonna pray like that in church before the tabernacle and then go and turn his heart to stone. You know it's hard out on those streets. Free as a bird ain't all it's cracked up to be. Man made sandwiches for the po' boy, but ain't make one yet for the po' girl. Your wife and baby miss me, too, ain't they?"

Cruz didn't answer. Whoever she thought he was now, she was accepting the moment. Una Vida walked into the house behind Cruz and Elvira. They held the door open for her as if she were royalty. She smiled at them graciously as she entered their home.

Cruz was thinking that Malta Park was an excellent idea and called immediately. The director promised to do his best to get Una Vida a room by Sunday, at least a temporary one. Cruz and Elvira could visit her in the evenings while he attempted to locate Jessica and learn what she could tell them about Una Vida's past. If he had to, he'd get Zevie to hire a private investigator. New Orleans wasn't that big, and Jessica wasn't the kind to leave town, he guessed. Everything was going to work out beautifully.

Elvira had ordered in food from around the corner and was transferring chicken, rice, and green beans from the plastic containers onto dinner plates at the kitchen table. She had even lit candles and put on a fresh royal-blue tablecloth. She told her husband that she was in the process of making up one of the kid's old rooms for Una Vida.

"She can stay here as long as she needs to," she added.

Cruz kissed his wife and squeezed her shoulder.

Chapter 9

A week had passed since they brought Una Vida home. It had been almost like having his mother with them again. Instead of singing on the levee, Una Vida walked around their fenced-in yard among the giant azaleas and hydrangeas, still singing her heart out – with a repertoire of classic songs that brought tears to their eyes when Cruz and Elvira happened to be within hearing distance.

"For the duration," Elvira had arranged to work from home. At the Center, Cruz focused on locating Jessica and on gently bugging the director about the place in Malta Park. Neither had yet produced results. No one on the street knew where Jessica was. She hadn't been home for at least a week, a neighbor said. Jessica owed two months' rent.

Cruz woke one morning to the sound of his cell phone ringing at 5:18. The clock's numerals shined brightly into his eyes as he reached for the phone. He left it on at night out of habit – from when the kids were young and out till all hours. It was Charity Hospital calling.

"Dr. Cruz," said a routinely calm voice on the other end of the line. "We have a woman who's barely coherent in the ER. She didn't have any ID, but she says her name is Jessica. We found your card in her pocket. Are you her physician?"

"I'm her friend," Cruz responded, suddenly wide awake. "Is she okay?"

"The officer that brought her in said he found an empty bottle of acetaminophen in her pocket and was inebriated. We're still trying to determine – "

Cruz cut the caller off. "I'll be right there."

He hung the phone up and reached for Elvira's hand. She was awake and had been listening to the call.

"It's Jessica," he said. "I have to go to the hospital."

"What's her status?" Elvira asked.

"She may have overdosed."

He kissed Elvira on the forehead, threw on some clothes, and made his way downstairs. As he was about to reach the front door, Elvira called to him from the top of the stairs.

"Whatever it is, Alvaro, it's not your fault. These people had lives long before you met them."

"I know," Cruz answered. "I know."

*

Unlike an overdose of certain narcotics or barbiturates, an overdose of acetaminophen, combined with an excess of alcohol, doesn't kill you quickly. It kills you over a period of four to seven days, and it does it painfully – by shutting down each of the vital organs in succession. If a cop hadn't brought Jessica in and she had continued holing up wherever she'd been hiding for a week, she would have suffered terribly and died an agonizing death.

Time was of the essence. The ER staff would have to act quickly to be sure the acetaminophen had not been absorbed internally. The remedy used to be standard stomach pumping, but now they gave a sort of charcoal milkshake: a thick black substance of horrible-tasting charcoal that acted to leech the medicine out of the body, pulling it away from the organs. The patient had to drink the concoction with a straw, which left the mouth and tongue black for days – but the patient survived.

Cruz was sure that the ER staff at Charity Hospital knew that, but he worried anyway. He showed his badge to the triage nurse at the ER entrance and let her know he'd been called. They let him through and told him that Jessica was in room 5B. The attending physician brought Cruz up to speed and showed him the acetaminophen bottle. He told Cruz that Jessica had started on the charcoal shake about twenty minutes ago and was sucking it down reluctantly. He asked Cruz if he wanted to talk to the officer who'd brought her in.

Cruz declined. He wanted to see Jessica first. He glimpsed the shoes of an ER nurse under the curtain and announced himself. The nurse opened the curtain and Cruz saw Jessica, drained of color, lying in the bed. She was conscious but groggy, and the nurse was speaking loudly to her, trying to keep her awake and drinking the black concoction. Jessica didn't recognize Cruz right away when he touched her cheek.

"She's going to be here a while," the nurse said.

Jessica's neck was having trouble holding her head up. Her left foot stuck out from the bottom of the white hospital blanket draped on top of her. It was filthy. Cruz had the urge to clean it. After realizing there was nothing useful he could do, he walked out to talk to the officer. The cop told Cruz he'd picked Jessica up in an alley behind Bourbon Street.

"At first I figured she was just slumped over like that because she'd had one too many, but when I poked her with my nightstick, I realized she wasn't moving. She was still breathing – barely." The cop spoke with the weary air of someone who'd seen it all more than a few times before.

Cruz thanked him and told him he probably saved her life.

"Part of the job," the cop replied. "Now let's see what she does with it; that's the trick. I save them, you save them, they save them here all night long; still, ten to one says I see her back on Bourbon in less than a week."

Cruz didn't answer the matter-of-fact observation and the policeman walked off. His shift had ended hours ago.

Out in the lobby, Cruz drank vending machine coffee that was both too weak and too hot, trying to clear his head, when he noticed a boy who couldn't have been more than four sitting in a child-sized chair at a child-sized table, drawing a picture. The boy seemed intent and unaware of the chaos around him: People with earaches, stomachaches, backaches, and toothaches, a man applying pressure to a bandage on his head, and a woman with her ankle wrapped. As far as the boy was concerned, it could have been the waiting room of a family doctor's office, complete with *People* magazine, *Newsweek*, and building blocks. The boy was oblivious to the fact that it was the New Orleans Charity Hospital Emergency Room or that a gunshot wound could come through the door any minute – and no doubt had within the past few hours.

Cruz went over to the boy and asked what he was drawing.

"A monster," the boy smiled.

"What kind of a monster?" Cruz asked.

"A friendly one," he said.

He was working with a yellow and green Crayola box of eight fat crayons that he grabbed one at a time and held in hand, like Churchill with an unlit cigar. He was working primarily in red, yellow, green, and blue. He was more sparing with black, purple, and orange, but made use of them as needed.

"You want to color?"

The boy looked up at Cruz and offered him a blue crayon. Cruz took hold of the crayon, folded his big body into the child-sized chair at the child-sized table and began to color. He had no idea why he was doing it, and he didn't care. He started to draw the sky above the monster's head. There wasn't a cloud.

The boy passed Cruz a yellow color as he got near the corner of the paper.

"Don't forget the sun," the boy said. "I'm going to give this picture to my sister when she comes out. She has asthma and can't breathe real good sometimes. This monster gonna help her breathe. You see how big his stomach is. That's air in there. And if my sister ever needs some, the monster could give it. We won't need to come to the hospital then."

The boy nodded with proud determination, and Cruz smiled without looking up as he continued to add rays to the sun on the page. Just as the picture was pretty well complete, the boy's mother flashed out of the swinging door. She couldn't have been more than twenty-four. Her hair was braided in short corn rows on top of her head and tied off at the bottom of her neck with purple and white beads.

"You can see Tamika now, Corey. Are you bothering that man?" the young woman added quickly.

"He's teaching me to draw," Cruz said, defending the boy.

The young woman wasn't listening. She simply pulled her son up and started putting his crayons away, then took him by the hand and headed out of the room. Corey turned to wave goodbye to Cruz before disappearing behind the ER door.

Cruz got up too, with a little more difficulty. Elvira

called his cell phone, and he told her what had happened and that the ER group had done everything properly so Jessica would probably be fine. Elvira told him that Una Vida had just woken up in splendid spirits and that the two of them were going to make pancakes together. She said she'd be fine and that Cruz should take his time. Cruz worried about his wife having her hands full, but soon dismissed the thought. She had handled untold crises, and he knew that better than anyone.

Cruz decided to check in at the Center and keep in touch with Jessica's progress by telephone. The hospital was just a pedestrian bridge away. He moved to the door and then looked back at the little table where he'd been working. In the commotion, Corey had forgotten his picture. Cruz picked it up and held it close as he walked outside the Emergency Room and passed the circular driveway until he got to the edge of the parking lot. An egg-orange sun was rising over the Crescent City, and all the possibilities, good and bad, of another day with it. The outline of the above-ground graves in the distance looked ominous and Cruz thought of Handsome John, wondering if he'd come through Charity's ER before passing on. He looked down again at the picture and thought about Corey and how he wished he could be looking up at that sun rise rather than down at the ER's scratched brown-and-gray asbestos floor.

*

Back at the Center, when he got to his office, Zevie told him his wife had called again.

"She's napping," Elvira told him when he returned her call. "I just thought I'd catch you up. Strangest thing happened when we were making pancakes," she continued. "I was cracking eggs and made a joke about hoping we didn't find any chicks inside the eggs, which got her to talking about Chick Webb. I didn't realize you had so many of his records."

Cruz loved Chick Webb – an African-American hunch-back dwarf who was probably the best jazz drummer of all time. He beat the bass drum so hard with his little foot that they had to nail his drum set down on stage to keep him from knocking it over.

"I've been playing your jazz records for her since break-fast, especially Chick Webb. I didn't realize Ella Fitzgerald wound up singing with his band. Una Vida's singing along with the records, Alvaro…it's unbelievable!"

*

When Cruz finally walked back to Charity Hospital, sheltered from the thundering rain by the covered bridge that connected it to his building, he was thinking about Una Vida responding to the ever-present moment of music and not having to respond to the past or to a future she was uncertain of. When the records ended, Elvira could just play them again and there the voices would be – as fresh and as perpetual as the sunrise. The thought made him smile. Maybe that was God's way of evening out the anguish.

His first order of business was to see if Corey was still there and return his drawing. It was after seven and the shift had changed, so Cruz had to go through the whole litany again with the newly-arrived triage nurse to get through the door. He peeked in all the rooms and skulked around the halls, but no Corey. No sign of his mother, either. Cruz thought about giving the picture to one of the nurses in case he came back for it, but thought otherwise and folded it neatly and put it in his pocket.

When he looked in on Jessica, she was sleeping with tubes of iv nutrients in her arm, though the nurse who'd phoned him had told him she was awake. Cruz thought of calling Elvira to check again, but thought better of it. He went out to the car to retrieve his briefcase so he could continue working on his next presentation. He settled into his chair with pen in hand. Just as he began editing the section on how important synaptic signaling in the hippocampus was because of its relationship to memory, Cruz was out like a light.

When a hospital gurney banged into the swinging doors and woke him, he couldn't believe the time. By the time Cruz got to Jessica's room, a consultant from the psych unit was just leaving. The IVs were out of Jessica's arm, her eyes were open, and she looked a world better. She also looked surprised to see him.

"Do you remember me?" he asked.

She nodded, flushed with embarrassment. "How did you know I was here?"

His eyes twinkled. "I have my spies everywhere," he said. "I'd been looking for you. I want to help Una Vida."

"I wish I could smoke in here."

Jessica was speaking in a perfectly even tone. Cruz had expected a slight slur at that point, but there wasn't any.

"What did she say?" he asked, motioning to the young psych nurse speaking to the attending physician outside the curtain.

"She asked me if I still felt like hurting myself. And she asked me if I was taking any medication."

"Well, do you?" Cruz asked.

"What?"

"Still feel like hurting yourself?" Cruz wanted to say "killing yourself," but couldn't get the words out.

Jessica looked different in a light-blue hospital gown under white covers, in a hospital bed in a room with oxygen in the corner. Everybody looks different in a room like that when stripped of their usual clothes and handed a sort of shroud to wear, Cruz thought.

"Why were you looking for me?" Jessica asked.

"You didn't answer my first question," Cruz pushed.

"I got stupid. Gave up a little bit, that's all."

"You call an entire bottle of acetaminophen plus who knows how many drinks a little bit?"

Jessica wouldn't meet his eyes.

"It's just a habit…the giving up. A bad habit when things start looking too hard. I didn't want to go back to coke or anything else back there, but I came close. And when you come that close to the door, where one more step inside could lead you to that dark, dank room of your old miserable life, you get the feeling that you want to cut it short. You don't want to see yourself heading down that road, and you don't know any other way to stop it."

By gentle but insistent questioning, Cruz got her to open up, first about her own pain, then about Una Vida's.

"I saw two roads," Jessica told him. "One was gonna kill me over time, and I'd have to watch myself become the person I despised, and the other one would just make an end of me quick, and at least I could go out with some dignity. I chose the quick."

Cruz had never thought of suicide as a dignified way to deal with pain, but in hearing Jessica's logic and the lack of options she'd felt, he understood what she was saying. He silently put his hand into his pocket and pulled out Corey's folded-up monster. He unfolded it and put it on the tray table that the nurse had rolled over to Jessica's bed.

"I met a boy out in the waiting room earlier. He drew this picture for his sister. He told me that this monster was of the friendly sort – a superhero that had just what his asthmatic sister needed. Whenever his sister's lungs didn't have enough air, this monster here, with all that air in his belly, could give her some so she wouldn't have to come to the hospital anymore to get oxygen," Cruz explained.

He flashed her a boyish grin and pushed the drawing toward Jessica's hand, bandaged now from where the IV had been. That gesture opened the floodgates. Jessica stared at the drawing, then turned her head to meet his eyes.

"I shouldn't have called that day for you to meet me outside the cathedral, Dr. Cruz. I didn't think you'd come; maybe part of me hoped you wouldn't. I hung up on your office without giving my name."

"Zevie knows when something is important," Cruz said.

Jessica let herself breathe naturally again at hearing that.

"I wish we could go back to that garden and try again."

"Let's pretend we're there," he said, pulling his chair closer to the bed.

"I hadn't been there since I was a kid," Jessica began. "My parents used to take me there all the time. I thought I'd be all right and that it made sense as a place to meet, but it had too big of an effect. I grew up around that church and not far from Ursuline Convent.

"My mother told me a story one time when we were there about how God spoke to her parents one rainy night some months before she was born. She sat me down in the pew where her mother sat and enacted the event of God's messenger putting her hand on my grandmother's shoulder. Mom burned that story into me over and over again until I didn't know anymore whether she had told it to me or I'd simply always known it.

"My grandparents had gone to the church to pray one Monday night. But they weren't religious, not in the usual way. It was dark and the last Mass was long over. It was January too, damp and cold. My grandmother had just been released from the hospital after giving birth to a stillborn. She thought God was punishing her for something."

As Jessica continued to talk, Cruz began to see her grandmother and experience the cave of memory revealed by the emotion in Jessica's eyes and clear voice. It was as if the past were spilling into the present through the portal of her being. He saw Jessica's grandmother get down from the pew and kneel in front of the pure white, intricately carved tabernacle adorned with angels that had the bodies and faces of babies. She shook her fist at the three statues above: Faith, Hope, and Love.

"What kind of God needs my baby?" she wailed. Jessica's grandfather stayed seated in the pew, his hands over his eyes. "What is all this for? These paintings and statues, these empty words of promise! I thought You were about the Word made flesh. Is it too much to ask You to spare the living flesh of one child? Have I been so horrid?"

Just then, when all felt lost, Jessica's grandmother felt a presence behind her. She shrugged it off at first, tired of consolation from a husband who didn't understand the anguish of carrying a baby for nine months in her womb only to see that in the end the world would not sustain her offering. The presence persisted in putting its hand directly on Jessica's grandmother's shoulder.

The presence was also crying as she softly spoke the words, "I'm sorry."

With those two simple words, Jessica's grandmother turned around and took hold of the girl standing before her and hugged her as if she were the angel Gabriel stepping out of eternity to comfort her.

The girl was thin as a rail, had sores in her mouth and bruises on her body. Jessica's grandfather stood and walked over, asking the girl where she'd come from and what she was doing there. The girl said she didn't have a home and that her place for sleeping was that church. The paintings, coming alive with the flickering of the votive lights, made her imagine she was in heaven and put her to sleep.

For Jessica's grandmother, God had finally spoken; that teenage girl had delivered His voice. She brought the girl home and gave her the room she'd prepared for the baby.

"And that girl sleeping in the church was Una Vida?" Cruz asked.

Jessica nodded. Three months after Una Vida went to live with Jessica's grandparents, her grandmother Ella got pregnant. Ella was put on bed rest for nearly the entire pregnancy. Una Vida put a fresh coat of paint in the nursery and drew a flower garden on the walls. Ella had asked her to make the space new so she'd never take to comparing how that baby was to how the stillborn baby might have been.

Una Vida sat on the side of the bed with Ella for three hours a day as they sewed clothes for the newborn. Una Vida was handy with a needle and thread and had an artist's eye for matching material. Her baby quilt picked up the red, pink, royal blue, green, and orange of the paints and flowers in the room, as well as the powder blue and white that she'd painted on the ceiling to depict a summer sky. The nursery was a breath of new life.

Una Vida also made it her business to get out early in the morning to go to the French market to pick out the best okra, cucumbers, green beans, mustard greens, and black-eyed peas and purple hulls – corn, too, when it was in season. And lots of fruit: apricots, watermelon, purple grapes, plums, apples, bananas, pears, oranges, lemons, limes, and peaches. She wanted to be sure that Ella got all the nutrients and vitamins she could possibly absorb. She even went out to the river from time to time to catch redfish and catfish with a cane pole, cork bobber, and straight hook.

And when Jack, Jessica's grandfather, could afford it,

she'd prepare pot roast, chicken and dumplings, and barbecue. Jack liked most of what Una Vida cooked for them, especially her cornbread, which he liked to eat as a meal if he could dip the pieces in a glass of buttermilk. Jack worked as a tourist driver, introducing visitors to the wonders of the city with his mule and carriage.

Cruz's face must have shown his surprise because Jessica interrupted her narrative to take his hand.

"Is something wrong?" she asked.

"He was a driver? You said his name was Jack?"

Jessica nodded. "John. Jack was a nickname that only the family used. Most folks called him 'Handsome John.'"

Cruz was stunned. The revelation that Jessica's grandfather was Handsome John made him feel like the designated witness to some kind of new galaxy that had been there all the while, but unnoticed.

"I'm sorry," he said. "He was a good man. He took my wife and me on his very last ride."

"I know," she said. "I saw you that night, remember?"

Cruz did remember, and he also suddenly recalled that John had told them, "She's all right," and that he hadn't quite understood the tone in John's voice. Now he did. It was the sound of a grandfather struggling with his feelings about the granddaughter he still loved despite her erring ways. He told Jessica what Handsome John had said about her.

She listened hungrily.

"I'd love to see your pottery," Cruz said.

"I'd love you to see it," she replied.

Chapter 10

Cruz urged Jessica to continue her memories. She said that Jack often came home sore and completely famished. After a good plate of Una Vida's cooking, he was ready for a hot bath, drawn by Jessica, a look at the sports page, and a night's sleep. But during her pregnancy, Ella insisted that Jack read the Bible aloud to her, Una Vida, and the baby in her stomach before he retired. He did it grudgingly at first, never having been much of a reader, but in time, the stories grew on him and he read them for their adventure more than for their morality. He liked to skip over the "lesson parts," as he called them, but Ella liked those parts best of all and wanted them recited again and again. Una Vida would draw pictures of what she heard and use them as shelf paper to line the drawers of the baby's bureau.

One in particular that Jessica's mother hung onto, and had framed when she was old enough, was a picture Una Vida drew of Joshua stopping the sun in the sky so he could keep the battle raging all day without the interference of nightfall. His left hand was open and stretched out to the sky as he used his right to wield his sword. Una Vida never tired of hearing of the supernatural, and the acts Jack read to her were as real to her as the sun rising each morning.

Ella went into labor one night after a meal of collard greens, sweet potatoes, and fried chicken. She told Una Vida that she wanted to wash the dishes and felt that the baby wouldn't come if she was lying down. Una Vida consented, and by the time the cast iron skillet had been scraped clean, Ella was in labor.

Jack called the midwife and Una Vida took to readying the house for a delivery. She'd bought a variety of herbs from the French market for the purpose of calming Ella at that moment and helping her body give in to the natural forces it needed to. Early on, Ella started to cry. Una Vida believed it was more than the physical pain making her cry; it was the mental anguish of believing she could give birth to another dead baby. Una Vida prepared a strong tea of the herbs and roots and made Ella drink it, despite its powerful smell. The concoction calmed her nerves and allowed her to settle down to the work of labor.

It was called labor for a reason; no one ever worked harder than a woman delivering a baby. Una Vida dipped towels into the water from the tea and rubbed the mixture all over Ella's body, especially her temples and her stomach. When Ella's fear gave way, she began to dilate naturally. By the time the midwife arrived from across town and checked her, she was doing fine.

Una Vida, who had prepared the bed with fresh sheets and firm pillows, continued massaging Ella's body as the herbs did their part and the midwife coached her forward. The pain was unbearable, and Una Vida prayed for it to be channeled into her so she could share its burden. Jack stood at the door like a bear about to claw himself if he didn't get news every ten minutes

By the time she was at eight centimeters and twenty-nine hours had passed, the midwife wanted to call in a doctor because Ella's strength was sapped to the point where she was afraid she wouldn't be able to push. When she heard what the midwife was saying, Una Vida grabbed tighter to Ella's hand and told her she could do it. She told her to bring the pain to her heart and let all the love for her child take over until that pain was transformed to strength. She told her of Sarah giving birth to Isaac at the age of 95. She told her of Mary bearing Jesus and the pain she had to endure. She told her that life comes from pain and struggle and that it was the women of the world who kept it going through their sacrifice. She told her all of that as a song she sang into her ear. She told it with the music of her own mother. Ella heard it and found her second wind deep inside herself. Without uttering another word until the midwife told her the baby had crowned, she did the work of labor and brought forth a life bigger than anything she'd ever imagined coming out of her.

When the midwife joyously reported the coming child, Ella perked up and spoke from the center of her being. "Let Una Vida's hands be the first to touch that child."

So Una Vida's large hands delivered the baby. Ella often recounted to Jessica how it was Una Vida's hands and voice that gave birth to Jessica's mother, Rose. She believed that Rose finally came out because she was lured by the sweetness of Una Vida's singing, a voice not even the devil could resist.

Within days, though, the reality hit that Rose wasn't well. It was nothing life threatening or damaging in the long term, but in the short term, Rose simply couldn't get comfortable. She had a bad case of the colic and howled almost constantly. Jack and Una Vida took turns walking Rose through the night, since that was the only thing that seemed to give her peace. Ella tried to rest between the long sessions of nursing.

It went on that way for close to six months and it was tearing Jack and Ella apart. Their saving grace was Una Vida. She was steadfast in her care for everyone in the house, like a ship's captain who never went off watch and never lost sight of the horizon. It took the better part of a year for Ella's strength to return and for her to begin taking over some of the chores of the house. She couldn't believe that Una Vida had been with them for more than two years and that she hadn't cooked a meal or changed a bed in all that time; she'd simply been flat on her back, waiting for the baby and then sitting up long enough to nurse her. She knew that it was only because of Una Vida that she had the life she did.

"You know what makes me the saddest?" Jessica suddenly asked Cruz. "My grandfather probably died thinking I was still an addict."

Cruz didn't know what to say, but it didn't matter. He thought again of Handsome John's statement, "She's all right." Jessica continued before he could speak.

"That's not true," she sobbed. "I'm lying. What broke me up and threw me into a tailspin was that I didn't have the guts to go to my own grandfather's funeral."

"You were taking care of life, and sometimes that's all we have the strength to do. You need to forgive yourself for this." His voice was thick with emotion. "Then we'll find a way for you to go on."

The hardness in her eyes melted.

"Everyone eventually gives up on you when you're an addict. They have a right to. But Una Vida never did. When she was well, she kept writing me letters in that backward scrawl of hers – kept writing whether I answered or not. I have stacks of them at home in a big folder. Those letters are my book of psalms. I should recopy them someday, type them out in a book," she spoke through tears.

"Una Vida's letters made sense for the longest time, and then gradually they didn't. She repeated things, but worse than that, she wrote all over the page. Her letters and words had always been off – I figured out a long time ago that she must've had dyslexia, but this was different. There was no rhyme or reason to it," Jessica continued. "Just stream of consciousness random, and that's never the kind of person she was. She was always deliberate, measured, and careful with her choice of words, just as she was when she was sing-ing and enunciating perfectly. I started to struggle to stay sober, hoping it was just me and the letters would make sense again once I got off the junk, which was messing with my head in a really bad way.

"Deciphering her letters and the crazy drawings she sent with them became an obsession that I connected to deci-phering the mess I'd made of my own life. I checked myself into a program for the last time. They say a drug addict has to touch rock bottom before she gets up. Her letters held me up. At the end of each letter she always said, 'Please let me stay or they'll take him away,' and 'I'm praying for you.' When you know someone is so concentrated on you for a protracted period of time, it has an effect. I'm not talking about guilt. It's more inviting than that. After a while I gave my life over to it, and I think I eventually quit using because giving myself over to Una Vida's vision of me was just big-ger than anything else. Once I got sober, the first person I started writing to was Una Vida. When I realized that her letters still weren't making much sense, I got up the cour-age to write my mother."

*

143

When Jessica walked through the door of the house she hadn't stepped into in twenty years, she was struck by its size. It was much smaller than she remembered, but it was also brighter. The walls had gone from dank green to bright yellow and blue. The old milk can on the front porch that she used to sit on had been relegated to the attic. As she walked around the place, the emotional charge it had over her mind dissipated. The smell of sickness and death permeated the place.

Rose, now just eighty-five pounds, lay in a hospital bed with tubes in her nose and an IV in her arm. She was on a morphine drip and slipped in and out of consciousness. At the sight of her, Jessica felt her knees buckle. She covered her mouth for fear she would vomit. A hospice worker quickly led her out of the room and got her a glass of water.

"You haven't seen your mother in a long time. She looks different, but she's still your mother," the heavyset nurse told Jessica. "She has her moments when she can speak as clearly as the day is long."

Jessica caught her breath after a few moments and walked back into the room. Her mother took note of her and motioned her over with the hand free of an IV.

"You're beautiful," were the first words Rose said to Jessica as she squeezed her hand with what little strength she had left.

In that space where daily life had gone and the mind lived on the precipice of death, the notion of time was let go. A day or twenty years could feel like the same interval if the familiarity of love was present. It was in that way that Rose experienced Jessica. No explanations were needed; all was forgiven.

Jessica spent that night in her childhood bedroom. It had been converted into a sewing room, and she slept on the floor on patchwork quilts that Una Vida had stitched together long ago. When she woke the next morning and went down to the kitchen to look for coffee, she heard a knock at the door. Still in her robe, she waited as the hospice nurse went to answer. Jessica figured it was the shift change for the nurse, but it wasn't. Within a moment, she recognized the voice of Una Vida.

With tears in her eyes, Jessica stepped out to get a look at Una Vida. Before she could speak, Una Vida grabbed hold of her like a child that had run away and come back just when everyone thought all hope was lost. Una Vida didn't say a word, save the tune she started to hum. Jessica didn't say anything either, just allowed herself to be held in this place of home. When Una Vida let go, she looked at Jessica squarely and hesitated.

"Are you my sister?" Una Vida asked through her tears.

"I'm Jessica."

"Yes, my baby sister."

Rose had known for some time that just as her own body was slipping away, so was Una Vida's mind – that most days when she came to visit, Una Vida inevitably forgot why she'd come, how she'd gotten there, or even where the kitchen was. Something was desperately wrong with Una Vida, but Rose didn't have the strength to help her. Just as Una Vida always had, she wanted to take care of others – even when she didn't fully know who they were. A mere sense of connection was enough.

On the fourth day of Jessica's first – and last – visit to her childhood home in twenty years, Rose wrapped both of her bony, translucent hands around Jessica's head in a moment of desperate clarity.

"God has brought you back," she said. "Now you must do His work. Una Vida is not well…you must see to her. She brought me into this world. My mother always told me how she sang me into this place. I imagine she'll sing me out as well, at least I hope she will. I never repaid her. No one in this family has ever repaid her. You must promise me that you'll make good on our family's debt."

Rose kissed Jessica with her cracked, colorless lips that tasted like a still pond where fish no longer swam. After that kiss, Rose fell back onto her bed – into a sleep that would be her last. Una Vida had wandered out and the hospice nurse told Jessica that her mother needed rest. Jessica felt the need then to return to her studio and do something with her hands. Emotion, without a creative channel to release it into, was dangerous for an addict. It threatened to overwhelm and wash away.

That evening Jessica took a fresh slab of clay, worked it with her wet fingers into a ball, placed the ball in the center of the potter's wheel, and began the process of centering an object without thinking about what she was doing. She let her mind go and allowed her hands to feel for a reality she felt the need to escape. Her hands and the wheel had their own relationship, and they were bound and determined to get at the truth, despite the reticence commanding Jessica's consciousness. She just turned her mind over to her hands and they produced the work.

By the time she finished, it had gotten late, and all of the energy of fear and anguish had dissipated and given way to the object that appeared before her. Jessica looked down at what she had done and felt at first as if her hands had betrayed her. She was angry with their knowledge and their need to realistically communicate what was happening. Her first instinct was to destroy their work, to mash it out of existence. But she didn't do that. Instead she looked at it and knew it was true enough to fire in the kiln and make permanent.

At that point in her story, Jessica broke off and lapsed into silence. Cruz allowed the silence to continue. She'd resume when she was ready. Little by little, he saw her face regain its composure.

"It was an urn," Jessica finally said.

"You made a vessel for your mother's ashes."

Jessica nodded. "Ironic, isn't it? I never invited the woman to stay in my house when she was alive, but in death I keep her on my desk in a container I threw, fired, and glazed with my own hands. My mother is more intimate to me in death than she ever was when she was alive."

Cruz realized he felt the same way. Now that his mother was no longer among the living, he told himself on that anguished flight from Rome to New Orleans, he'd be able to give her a permanent shrine in his mind – a tabernacle where she was exactly as he best remembered her and would never change. Now he realized it would be okay – it would even be better, in fact – if he remembered her not ideally, but as she was. It was okay to accept the imperfection of humanity – of his mother. Even of himself.

"I did what she asked, as long as I could stand it," Jessica went on, breaking into tears. "But Una Vida doesn't even know who I am. I had her drawings, her letters, some of her jazz records, but she doesn't know me. Sometimes she thinks I'm somebody else, but most times I'm just a stranger. I couldn't stand it. Then Stompleg gave me your card, and my mother's voice came into my head. 'Everything happens for a reason,' she always told me."

Unbidden, his mother's voice drowned out Jessica's.

"Follow your dream."

It was what the woman wearing Shalimar was saying in his dream. But he suddenly remembered it was also the words his mother had said when he explained his desire to study neuroscience and to understand the brain. She never wavered in her support of his ambition to excel in his field. Even when he failed to be at her side when she, hidden deep inside that shell of nonentity that Alzheimer's created, may have needed him the most.

"Are you listening?" Jessica asked.

"Yes, I'm sorry," Cruz replied.

"So I thought you had come down to the river for a reason," she went on. "That woman out on the river who barely knows her own name saved my life." Jessica was out of breath and the tears came without signs of stopping. "You're a doctor, a neuroscientist. You know what this is... Alzheimer's, and it's progressing. She's being lost. Can you help me talk to her? Can you help me get her to know me again, to remember my grandparents and what she did for them? Just so I can thank her, and she can hear me? If you do that, I'll be forever in your debt."

She waved the monster drawing at him.

"I didn't know you were such a fine artist," Jessica smiled for the first time. "It'd be good to have something around to give you air when you feel like you can't breathe."

She then quickly sneezed three times in a row, tilting her head away from the picture. Cruz passed her a tissue and she blew her nose.

"Are you coming down with a cold?"

"You'd think all those painkillers I took would be good for something," Jessica said, letting her smile open to laughter.

Cruz laughed, too, and felt glad. The nurse came in, bringing Jessica ice chips.

"If the blood test comes back right, you'll be going home soon," she said brightly.

Jessica accepted the small Styrofoam cup. "This must be the secret cure-all," she said to Cruz, "because it seems like no matter what you have, the first thing they bring you in the hospital is ice chips." She took some ice in her mouth.

"They do feel good going down your throat, though. Always taste better than the kind you make at home."

Cruz suddenly realized he was hungry and told Jessica he'd be back to take her home when she was discharged. She told him that wouldn't be necessary.

"I know that," he told her. "Let me do it anyway."

He turned to leave.

"Wait," Jessica sputtered. "Una Vida," is all she got out at first. "Can I see her?" she finally managed.

Cruz turned around, facing her. He hadn't wanted to burden her with anything, hadn't thought it right to bring up anything that might make for a difficult moment, but there it was. Actually, he was glad she was aware enough to think of Una Vida.

"She's at my house, probably still eating pancakes and singing Ella Fitzgerald to my wife," he said. "We picked her up last night and took her home with us."

"So she's all right?" Jessica asked.

"She's fine." Then he met her eyes. "You'll see for yourself. When I come to pick you up later we'll all have a meal together. Everything's going to be okay now, Jessica. We're all going to work together to make a fresh start for everyone," Cruz said.

"I could use a fresh start," Jessica said, her bandaged hand now resting on the metal table on top of the picture of Corey's monster.

Cruz went over and gently placed his hand on top of her bandaged one. "I'll see you soon," he whispered, looking into her eyes, seeing a fire he thought no amount of pills could possibly burn out.

*

When Cruz pulled up to the house, things seemed incredibly quiet. He walked in and saw Elvira sitting on the floor

149

reading the liner notes on a Billie Holiday album. Her eyes were red. A record was on the turntable but wasn't playing. Una Vida was standing in the center of the room, her clarinet beside her.

"What is it?" he asked.

"I've never heard the song played that way before," Elvira said.

When Cruz went to the record player and saw what was on it, he was sorry he hadn't thought to warn Elvira to stay away from such a tune, the kind that hit too close to home for Una Vida and sent the neurons to firing a story of who knew what. He took the record off the turntable, took the album jacket out of Elvira's hands, and put the record away. He thought that would be the end of it. But he was wrong. Something in Una Vida had already been touched. She began to sing again, even as Cruz sealed the album up and turned it around so the label was out of sight.

It was as if Billie Holiday had been channeled into their living room to sing the words more piercingly than ever before. Something about the terrible beauty of the moment frightened her. He'd learn only later from Parker that Billie Holiday first sang what became one of her signature songs, "God Bless the Child," at Café Society in Greenwich Village, New York in 1938 where she performed three shows a night before an integrated audience. The owner of Café Society, where Holiday performed solidly for nine straight months, was a man by the name of Barney Josephson, an ex-shoe salesman who believed in the dignity and vision of jazz. To him, Billie Holiday was a street prophet who spoke a truth beyond color, time, or place.

As Cruz stood in his living room watching the two women and hearing the music, his insides were burning – as if he were drinking the black charcoal concoction that Jessica had had to sip that morning; a taste of death to wake you to life. Remarkably, even though the record was hidden away on the shelf, it lived in the flesh of Una Vida's memory. Had Una Vida been there to hear Billie Holiday at Café Society?

Billie's story was so much like Una Vida's that he marveled at the parallels. Billie's father died violently and tragically. She ran away from home at the age of twelve or thirteen, started singing for extra money in the brothel parlors where she worked washing floors and steps, and listening to the likes of Louis Armstrong. In 1933, Billie was thirteen, the same year Una Vida came to New Orleans at the age of fifteen. By the time Una Vida got to the last stanza of the song, Cruz was certain. Certain indeed that Holiday had sung the song one night and burned it right into Una Vida, to be remembered for all time. And it would be forever imprinted into Cruz and Elvira's memories, as well, as if the ink on the paper the words had been written on had still been wet.

From brain to brain, axons travel a path of unpredictable reach. They let us touch the minds of those who came before us and ignite their original passion in our own minds. History is pure biology. This is the true regeneration of neurons – the eternal outreach of one mind that we can keep collecting, refining, borrowing, rejecting, and making our own until it's time to pass it on to the one who needed it even more.

As suddenly as she'd begun, Una Vida stopped singing. She looked around the spacious living room, entirely lost. Then she looked at Elvira with something resembling recognition in her eyes.

"That baby's already asleep, ain't she?" she said. "Sure she is. Child like that need her rest, growing like she is. Miss, you went and cooked this meal and you shouldn't of.

I'm going to be doing all of that again now. Let me at least make the tea."

Elvira took the outburst in stride. Leaving Cruz to his thoughts, she led Una Vida to the teapot, the kettle, and the sugar, and pointed to the ice in the freezer so she'd have what she needed to make iced tea.

Cruz was trying to pinpoint whether Una Vida had been talking about Ella's child, Rose, or Rose's child, Jessica. Or, as he'd suspected before, did she herself have a child of her own who'd been somehow lost along the way?

Elvira came back and told Cruz that she'd reheat the food for him once the tea was ready. After making a stop in the bathroom, Cruz went into the kitchen to see how Una Vida was doing. She was staring at a pitcher with sugar, a tea bag, and ice in it – staring and smiling.

"Just waiting on this tea."

Elvira was busy warming the food. There was no water boiling on the stove, so Cruz filled the kettle in the sink and put it on the stove. Sometimes Elvira was absent-minded.

"What you doing that for?" Una Vida asked.

"For tea," Cruz said.

"Here I am making iced tea," she said, "and you decide now you want hot tea…ain't that just like a man?"

"We need boiling water for both, don't we?" Cruz said.

"Since when? I ain't never heard of that, Bird."

"Did you just call me Bird?" Cruz stopped and looked at her.

Una Vida looked confused. Then her eyes went blank.

"Why don't we just eat the food while it's hot? We can drink tea after," Cruz suggested.

Una Vida walked out of the kitchen and took a place at the table, where she began trying to eat her string beans with a knife. Cruz hadn't noticed any motor problems at Maspero's when they ordered roast beef po'boys, but then again, there hadn't been any utensils on the table to choose from, and Elvira had reported that she was perfectly capable of taking a shower, combing her hair, and dressing herself. Elvira asked her to pass the knife, but Una Vida looked blank.

When Elvira pointed at the utensil in her hand, Una Vida looked down and said, "This sharp thing?" as if she had never heard the word before.

Elvira said she needed it and left Una Vida with only a fork, which she proceeded to use as a sort of shovel with her right hand as two fingers on her left hand acted as a broom. Una Vida became quiet and after eating began to strain at the table.

Elvira understood the signal quicker than Cruz did and got her off to the bathroom. She stayed there with her and talked her through the parts she was forgetting. Confronted with them for the first time, the practical realities were worse than Cruz had imagined. He thought of Stompleg and Jessica dealing with the daily necessities that hadn't crossed his mind until that moment because Una Vida had manifested such strong functionality. He was convinced that her music had retarded the disease, though it wasn't something he could prove without examining her frontal cortex. But if proven, it represented a significant finding. A ray of hope, signaling breakthroughs, might lie just over the horizon.

Cruz made hot tea for everyone and they sat down together in the living room to drink it. Una Vida directed the conversation his way.

"I been thinking about what you said," she began. "About me wasting my time on jazz and how you were saying I had the talent to play classical like you once did. Soon as I woke up in your car, I made up my mind to learn, if you're still of the mind to teach me. Maybe you're right about all that.

Got these new reeds in my pocket and I reckon tomorrow
we can try 'em out."

"What was it I said about jazz?" Cruz asked.

"You told me to forget about it. I know I promised last
night not to mention the word. I know the ones who com-
pose it ain't the kind of educated men you want me to learn
on. I know that and I'm gonna change it. I'm gonna learn
that music like you want it played and I'm gonna come to
Birdland and make you proud. That's all I'm a mind to do."

"We don't need to talk about any of that now," Cruz heard
himself say, as if reading from a script. "You're home and
that's what matters."

Elvira smiled at Una Vida and they all sipped their tea.

"Guess I'll be turnin' in now. You done wore me out,
mister. Lot to do in the morning...I reckon that baby be
wakin' up early."

Una Vida stood and Elvira stood, too.

"It's been a long day for everyone," Elvira said. "Let me
walk you to your room so we can sit a minute. I might have
moved your nightgowns since you left."

Elvira walked Una Vida upstairs and Cruz went to the
phone to call Malta Park's director. He apologized for bothering him at home on a Friday night and related the situation. The director told Cruz to hold while he checked with
the St. John's unit. He came back on the line quickly and
told Cruz there was still no room, but it looked hopeful for
next week.

"That patient you met here the other day took a turn for
the worse and might have to be moved to the hospice unit,"
the director said. "The next person on the waiting list hasn't
been called yet. If you want it, it's yours."

Cruz thanked him and put the phone down, suddenly
weary. Jessica popped into his mind. He didn't want her to
try to talk him out of anything. He told himself he wasn't

calling her to spare her the worry over something she couldn't do anything about at the moment. Elvira came back downstairs.

"I gave her one of Maria's old nightgowns. She asked for a satin pillow. I told her it had been sent out to be cleaned. Who does she think we are and where does she think she is?" Elvira asked, as if Cruz knew the answer.

"She can probably have a room in Malta Park in a week; Raymond's father won't be needing it anymore." They exchanged a look of sympathy, and he could see Elvira wasn't surprised by the news. "She'd start getting the care she needs there. Living on the street or wherever she's been has just been adding to the stress of her disease. I think it must be making it worse. From what I know, I believe she thinks we're Jessica's grandparents and that I kicked her out of the house for some outlandish reason and have brought her back, but I'm not sure."

"You think Jessica knows?" Elvira asked.

"I think she knows a lot," Cruz said. "From what she's already told me, her family's story is completely entwined with Una Vida. We're going to find out just how much tomorrow. We're going to tell the people at Malta Park about it and we're going to help her have as much peace as possible."

Cruz spoke with a sense of determination in his voice. He was feeling incredibly protective; part of him was defensive about shuttling Una Vida off, and part of him was panicking about having to keep her for a week. But he knew he could handle it.

"It's like we're all actors in a play she wrote, but none of us know our lines and just have to improvise off hers," Elvira said.

Cruz was silent as he let that idea sink in. Later that night he began to think that Elvira's description of improvisation could be true for anybody. All people enact plays in their heads that correspond to their thoughts, feelings, emotions, cognitions, and histories. Human beings externally act out an internal drama again and again and often leave the real people in their wake dumbfounded by how they didn't listen and merely heard what their biases expected to hear.

Elvira soon walked Cruz up to bed and told him how much the night at the Cornstalk Inn had meant to her. They brushed their teeth with their own toothbrushes, washed, undressed, and got into bed. Cruz was exhausted.

*

Sometime around 3:00 A.M. Cruz was awakened by screams and by Elvira grabbing his hand. He jumped out of bed, as if his reflexes were still set on automatic to run to a child's room. But this wasn't a child. It was Una Vida.

When Cruz and Elvira got to her room, she was sitting up in bed, sobbing. He turned on the small light at her bedside and caught sight of a face torn in anguish – a poignant incarnation of the Goya painting.

"Don't take my baby away from me. Ain't no reason to do that. I can provide for him. Let go of him, let go! Let go! No, no, no…"

Una Vida gripped the pillow with both her large wrinkled hands, her eyes taking in a vision of the apocalypse. Then her eyes met Elvira's.

"Make them go away! Make them go away! Don't let them take my baby from me. Not my baby! Not my baby! I don' want my baby livin' in no cornfield."

She smoothed the pillow and began to rock it. Then she started to sing:

You show your sympathy dear, to every bird indeed
　　But when it comes to me you laugh at every plea.

Sweet Lord I need the bliss…

Then she just hummed the tune to the pillow in her arms, caressing it like a child. Elvira went to fetch a glass of water as Cruz sat on the bed next to Una Vida and put his arm around her shoulder.

"It's going to be okay," he said. "It's going to be okay."

He made small invisible circles with the palm of his hand on her back, the way he had when one of his children woke up in the middle of the night from a bad dream. He slowly guided her body back around to a prone position after a while and tucked the pillow back under her head. She was docile as she sipped the water. Elvira put a warm towel on her forehead and then went quietly went back to their room. Cruz remained sitting on the edge of the bed until Una Vida drifted asleep.

"Baby Have Pity on Me," the song Una Vida had been singing, brought tears to Cruz's eyes every time he heard it. Bessie Smith had recorded it for Columbia Records in 1930. But never had it sounded so powerful. When he returned to bed, he told Elvira that Una Vida had fallen back asleep.

"She did have a child," he said. "I'm sure of it. She was afraid they'd take him to a cornfield. What could that mean?"

Chapter 11

When Cruz got to Charity Hospital, Jessica was sitting in the ER waiting room wearing clothes three sizes too big for her. The hospital had given them to her, in light of how dirty and ripped the ones she'd come in wearing were. She wanted to go home to her studio to change, and then she wanted to see Una Vida.

The car ride to her studio on Elysian Fields was mostly silent, except for her telling Cruz where to turn. She was precise and gave him plenty of notice, not assuming he knew where he was going. Before he knew it, they were on a familiar street they'd come to in a way Cruz never would have chosen on his own. He had driven there, but only in the sense that he had held the wheel and depressed the pedals.

He waited downstairs by the potter's wheel in her studio while Jessica went up to change. Among what looked like the most recent batch of cups and vases, Cruz noticed a small as yet unfired sculpture of two dancers. He carefully picked up the piece to get a better look. The male was swinging the female around. Their right hands were clasped; their left hands flew free and high above their heads. Their feet glided on the ground.

When Jessica came down to find Cruz with the dancers in his clumsy hands, he felt as if he had just been caught reading someone's diary.

"I was just thinking about those notes and pictures of Una Vida's that I sent you. You haven't mentioned them."

Jessica now looked much more like the intriguing persona Cruz had first met in the courtyard of St. Anthony's garden. She had Corey's picture in her hand and tacked it up over her drafting table. Cruz carefully put down the sculpture.

"I have them at home. I'll give them back to you this evening," he said. "I'm not sure if they provide much in the way of answers, I'm afraid," he continued as he made his way toward the door. He took out his car keys.

"That's disappointing." Jessica sat down on the tall metal stool in front of the drafting table. "I thought they would've told you something. Doesn't every object somebody makes tell you something about them?" Jessica looked down at the two dancers Cruz had just been handling.

"Maybe to some extent," Cruz answered.

Jessica picked up the clay dancers. "I was making this for Una Vida. I hadn't had a chance to fire them yet. She was watching a show on my little TV there, and it had people dancing. All of a sudden she started talking about the Savoy Club in Harlem in the 1930s, when everybody was dancing the Lindy Hop. She said that went on into the beginning of World War II, and the dancing – what she called swinging – helped keep the spirits of the country up. She said the Savoy was closed in 1943 by the federal government because they claimed soldiers were contracting social diseases there. But Una Vida said the real reason the government closed the club was because everybody danced together regardless of their background. How can she not remember me but remember that club closing in 1943?"

After the Savoy shut down, jazz left Harlem for 52nd Street in Manhattan between 5th and 6th Avenue. Clubs like Three Deuces, Famous Door, and even one that bore the namesake of Charlie Parker's moniker – Birdland – opened and played jazz in crowded smoky rooms where the postwar generation didn't dance but just sat back and bopped.

"Do you know anything about Una Vida having a baby?" Cruz asked, surprising himself with the bold and unrehearsed question.

"Why would you ask me that?"

"Did she?" Cruz pressed again.

"I lost track of her for a long time," Jessica said, oddly looking away. "Are we going to see her?"

She stood up and checked her watch. The look on her face and the contortion of her mouth said she felt trapped. The rabbit wanted to dart away.

"She's at my home right now," Cruz said, letting it go for the moment. "Next week we're checking her into Malta Park, where they can take proper care of her."

"Do you really think she'll be happier in a place that'll keep her from going to the levee to sing?" Jessica's voice was shrill. "They'll never let me take her home! Once you get official people involved, it's all out of your hands. How could you do that without checking with me?"

Cruz told her about Stompleg and reminded her of her own plans, which certainly didn't include ever seeing Una Vida again, as far as he could tell. He was shifting responsibility away from himself and back in her direction. His tactic was working

"Why can't you just keep her home with you for a few more days till I'm on my feet?" Jessica finally said calmly.

Cruz didn't answer.

Jessica put on her coat.

"We'll figure the right thing out; the right thing for everybody," he finally said.

"Listen, Doctor, I appreciate all the good deeds you've done. I'm glad for it and I thank you." That was the most coldly formal tone she'd ever used with Cruz, and it came as a surprise. "I'm happy for Stompleg, too, but neither of you knows why I have to be the one to help Una Vida. I have to be the one!" Jessica was shouting again.

"I know the promise you made your mother – " Cruz started to recount the tale as best he knew it, but Jessica cut him off. Her voice dropped an octave.

"No, you don't know. You have no idea what that promise means."

"Then tell me," he demanded.

"You'd never understand what I'm talking about, so why bother?"

"So that's how you make sure you do everything alone?" Cruz snapped. "You never give anyone else a chance to come in?"

"I *am* alone," Jessica snapped back.

"But you don't have to be," Cruz offered, softening his tone. "I'm standing here beside you."

"Fine!" Jessica said.

Cruz unconsciously picked up the dancers again.

"I made those dancers for her. When I got into researching that time in the 1940s, I became fascinated with somebody named Charlie Parker. He never stayed in bounds. He went off into a universe that no jazz musician before him had ever seen or traveled to. He didn't believe in limitation. He'd be up there playing his solo, sweating with his eyes closed in some distant space, and the other musicians that came to watch their master would call out to him, 'Reach,

Bird, reach…' And he would. And he always got more as he reached out for notes and chord changes that were beyond anything that had ever been imagined, let alone played."

Jessica broke off, and reached for a cup of tea. Cruz didn't say anything. He just continued to stare down at the little clay people shaped by hands to dance. He dreamed of attacking science the way Bird had jazz. James Watson and Francis Crick conducted that kind of science in 1953, when they discovered the structure of the double helix. They heard the call of the scientists that walked the road before them: "Reach, reach…"

None of that mastery kept Charlie Parker warm at night and off the junk. None of it kept him from dying at thirty-four, just a year after he got the news that his two-year-old daughter had died of pneumonia. Our universal drive can only carry us so far before the personal creeps up and grabs hold of us, demanding the attention and resolution it so craved.

Cruz pulled himself back from his ramblings and made himself focus on Una Vida; what she'd meant to him since he first met her on the river. She was his second chance. Since he'd arrived in New Orleans, Cruz had struggled to remain focused on the universal, on science. He'd had a lab to build, a neuroscience center to organize where nothing had existed previously but empty rooms. His task had seemed overwhelming, but he worked at it looking only ahead, never back. He felt as if he hadn't caught his breath in twenty years. It was Una Vida, with her lack of coherent memory or sense of place and origin, who had prompted him to recall his own sense of place and the history attending it. It was Una Vida who'd put him back on track with himself and with life. The whole episode was much more than just science. In Una Vida's memory loss, Cruz saw the shadow of his own – the many years he'd spent focused on the brain, allowing the human being behind it to slip away to the point that he'd been looking the wrong way when his mother died.

Jessica had finished her tea. "One way or the other, even if it wasn't right on the flesh of the skin, lots of us saw people with a special reach on them and didn't do a thing to erase it. My mother lived with a vision of that, and she passed it on to me."

Jessica weighed the look of understanding in Cruz's eyes, and accepted it. With that, Cruz's jacket came off and his keys went back into his pocket. He called Elvira to tell her they might be a little while. Jessica excused herself from the room. When she returned, she was carrying a cardboard box; she dumped its contents onto the floor.

"There are over a hundred letters here," she said. "My grandmother never stopped loving Una Vida like a daughter. To her, she was always her eldest child. The two of them never lost touch," Jessica whispered as she spread the letters out, inviting Cruz to have a look.

Most of the envelopes were intact and Cruz ran his fingers over the addresses and read the postmarks. New York City, 1938, Paris, 1952, Los Angeles, 1955, Kansas City, Chicago, 1937, and every city in between were marked on the yellowing envelopes. No doubt Una Vida had lived on the road and followed the jazz, or more likely, had *been* the jazz that was followed. She'd lived as free as a bird, borne aloft by the wings of music.

"My mother never stopped getting letters from this woman and she never helped her." Jessica took hold of a letter that was worn from being handled and began to read the backward letters and the misspelled words of Una Vida's hand. Cruz could see it was postmarked January 12, 1940, Lafayette, Louisiana. "I'm sorry I didn't tell you this before."

Cruz raised his eyebrows.

Jessica read:

The City Office of Child Services coming to take my boy today. They said they was sending him to a home in Io-way! Said I wasn't sending him to school on account of my traveling for the jazz. But I was learning him on the road as best I could. A mother can only do what she can and I was gonna get enough money to get off the road next year and put him back in school but I don't have the money now. Could you write them and tell them that we are going to live with you in your house so I could send Parker to school there and maybe work steady in one of the old time clubs in the Quarter?

The letter continued, but Jessica stopped reading and began folding it back into the weathered creases and returning it back to the box – a ritual she had obviously performed many times. But Cruz had a sense that it was the first time it had been performed in front of anyone outside the family. Reading it to an outsider had broken a silence that both ripped at Jessica and relieved her.

"The letters after that came fast and furious for about a year until Una Vida finally began to believe, as everyone was telling her, that her son could have a better home with someone else."

"So she *had* a son. What was his name?"

"I don't remember," she said matter-of-factly. "I think that's when she got on drugs."

"Why didn't you tell me when I asked you?"

"I figured it was her business. I didn't know how serious you were about helping her." She smiled. "Letters started again when she got clean. Pictures came, too. She was painting, playing music, and living without her son. She stopped mentioning him, but painted him."

"Who was the father?"

Jessica shook her head. "Don't know. She always claimed he was conceived without one!" She laughed. "Said he was a kernel planted at the Cornstalk Inn." She laughed again.

Cruz's heart raced. His brain started spinning through a Rubik's cube of possibilities, trying to fit the pieces of coincidence, serendipity, and synchronicity into a meaningful pattern. But it still stubbornly eluded him.

"It made my grandmother sick, but she never spoke of it. Not until the end."

Jessica was letting it all spill out. There could be no returning to pretense or avoidance.

"Why didn't she help?" Cruz asked, as if such questions were simple ones, though he knew they weren't – and *never* were.

Jessica paused and drew in her breath.

"It's a long story," she said. "Let's just say she was disappointed in Una Vida."

They waited there a minute and then Jessica got up and pinched off a small piece of clay from a covered bin in the studio's corner. She sat back down to talk as she worked the clay in her hand.

"My grandfather, Handsome John, was Creole. My great grandmother on his side was a free person of color in the city of New Orleans. Back then, you had your Europeans, your free people of color – most of them Creole – and your slaves. Shades of color made a big difference in New Orleans. My grandfather's people were free people of color before the Civil War. But he was born in 1900, after the country's Jim Crow laws came to New Orleans.

"After the Emancipation Proclamation, all people of color were free, in theory. In reality, Jim Crow made everyone of color the same, and for my grandfather's people the Civil War was the worst thing that could've happened. His parents lost their status, their money, their land, and ev-

166

ery privilege they once had under the city of New Orleans color laws.

"At one time the city of New Orleans had these separate orchestras. They had a White Symphony Orchestra and a very prestigious Creole Symphony Orchestra. My grandfather's father had been a first violinist in the Creole Orchestra. He was wealthy, respected, and sure of himself. He thought that an intelligent European city as cultured as New Orleans would simply ignore the 'separate but equal' Jim Crow laws. He had a good friend by the name of Homer Adolph Plessy, also a Creole of color, who wanted to prove the laws wrong once and for all.

"Plessy boarded a 'Whites Only' train car in New Orleans and was arrested, tried, and convicted for breaking the law in 1892. Plessy took his case all the way to the Supreme Court in 1896 and lost. The U.S. Supreme Court confirmed that 'separate but equal' was constitutional."

Jessica centered the ball of clay on the turning wheel and began shaping a bowl.

"The special status of the New Orleans Creole community was erased overnight. The orchestra was disbanded and their voting rights were stripped. The law came down that if your grandfather had been a slave, you couldn't vote. Before Plessy v. Ferguson, ninety-five percent of New Orleans blacks were registered voters, but after that only one percent of them were eligible to vote."

Jessica was deep into the rhythm of her work and the history spilled out of her without pause.

"My grandfather grew up on stories of better times. His father had had a taste of freedom and privilege before Plessy v. Ferguson, and those memories had a profound effect on my grandfather. By the time my grandfather was born – he was the last of eight – his father had become a bitter drunk. Lots of his friends from the Creole Symphony Orchestra made a living by learning jazz and playing the local clubs and brothels. Jelly Roll Morton was Creole. But my grandfather's father wouldn't hear of it. He thought it was below him and he hated jazz. He banished it from the house and drank himself to death. But before the end, when my grandfather was still young and his father had times of sobriety, he taught my grandfather to play the violin in a classical way and made him swear that he would never play jazz with 'those hoodlums in the whore houses.' He told him he was too good for it, that the laws would change someday and a classical violinist would be needed again, and that when the laws changed he should be ready."

"What happened? How did he go from classical violin to driving a buggy?" Cruz wanted to know.

Jessica smiled and shook her head in a kind of philosophical disgust. "Can you imagine? He taught my grandfather to hate the only kind of music that would have him. When the New Orleans Orchestra rejected him because he wasn't the right color, my grandfather threw his violin into the river, watched it float away, and picked up a whip instead. He never played music again."

"So where does Una Vida fit into all that?" Cruz asked.

"Una Vida was just there and like most of us, found herself embroiled in something that didn't have the slightest thing to do with her personally. When my grandparents took her in as a sign and found religion that night at the foot of the tabernacle in St. Louis Cathedral, Jesus didn't wash away all the stories in my grandfather's soul. My grandfather wouldn't let anybody in on those stories – the private musings between a son and the father he loved – he held onto them and believed them like a private declaration of war he had sworn to uphold long before. Long before he had a wife and life of his own...long before he met Una Vida."

Jessica turned the wheel off for a minute, went to the

sink for a glass of water, and drank it all at once. She had worked all the air out of her clay and had smoothed it into the beginning of a perfectly round container. She sat back down by the potter's wheel, turned it on again, and continued to talk above the hum of the motor as her fingers concentrated on the object before her. Hands a little shaky, she picked up a small tool and began to shave off tiny ribbons of clay that dropped rhythmically to the floor of her studio.

"Maybe he wanted to love her just as she was – a gift from God, as they believed. But he couldn't help but feel betrayed by the jazz in her. He feared the sense of being okay with the music just as it was, of being proud even. When he arranged the clarinet lessons for her, it was for the sake of something classical; it was for his father, to honor him.

"When Una Vida developed her own talents and likes and dislikes and found her love in jazz, my grandfather kicked her out of the house and my grandmother was too weak to defy him, though she kept a secret vigil and got the mail every day and hid the letters like they were Anne Frank's own diary. She passed them on to my mother and my mother to me, but I was too selfish to do anything with it until now," Jessica finished.

"Is it for you to fix the mistake of your grandfather?" Cruz asked.

"Who else? My family kicked her to the curb once; I can't stand to repeat it," Jessica said as the smooth clay with ribbons missing in different spots revolved perfectly, spinning too fast to note what could have been even the slightest flaw. With each revolution, the wobbliness diminished and the roundness and rightness emerged.

"That's all ancient history," Cruz said. "What about what Una Vida needs right now? Malta Park isn't kicking her to the curb. You got help. You sought me out and now she's getting the best care, from my wife. Una Vida doesn't remember all the things you're saying now. It's gone, and you'd be better off letting go."

"She does remember," Jessica said. "Whether or not it comes out in proper order and form, she remembers it. Same way I could read all the meaning in her letters despite all the misspelled and backward words all those years, all the lack of punctuation; I still saw the meaning in them. It's the same way with this disease she's got. The memories are there and I hear them even when she doesn't. She just doesn't know how to connect them all with herself."

Jessica's fingers were wet and purposeful. There was a time when that is all he would have seen, but Cruz saw much more at that moment.

"So this is about you and your family, after all – not what's best for Una Vida now. What if I told you I thought you were still being selfish," Cruz said, not knowing exactly why he said it, except that maybe that line of reasoning would help.

Jessica started to shake her head. "I don't know why I'm about to tell you this, but you're the one who picked me up from the hospital after I tried to kill myself, so I guess you're going to hear it. I told you it was just Una Vida's letters that got me off the drugs, but it wasn't just that. When I couldn't understand the letters anymore, I decided to bring them to Amité, a tarot reader in front of the church, after I got off of work one night. She's known to be able to contact the dead."

"I met her," Cruz said. "At your grandfather's funeral. She read the cards for me." He laughed. "She called you the rabbit."

For a brief second, Jessica's face reflected the exact scared look Cruz had seen as she exited the garden that day to disappear into the crowd on Pirate's Alley. Then it resumed the calm expression she'd held while telling Cruz her story. She turned down the speed on the potter's wheel and watched it as it came to a stop. A small perfect bowl was on the wheel – a sort of Japanese rice bowl with seven perfect grooves layered into it without anything to hold onto.

"I told Amitė of my family's history with Una Vida and asked her what these letters were trying to say to me. She told me that if I didn't…if I couldn't make things right with her, then my grandparents and parents would continue to suffer on the other side."

Jessica paused and looked away. She carefully picked up the bowl and placed it on a wooden shelf with other pieces awaiting firing and glaze. Cruz was silent.

"I know you're a scientist and don't give credence to any of that, but I do. Una Vida may not exactly remember all that was done, but the air on earth and what lies beyond it certainly does." Jessica spoke without the slightest bit of doubt.

"So why kill yourself?" Cruz asked.

"I guess it all just seemed like too much just then. I thought I could barely manage responsibility for my own life, let alone the souls of my family," Jessica said. "I figured I might as well join them, in whatever state."

Cruz maintained composure. "So what's changed now?" he asked.

Jessica was much calmer since her bowl had been made and the story was out of her. She was resigned to the analysis of Amitė Deerkill, regardless of what Cruz or anyone else thought. She allowed herself to take a confident independent distance from him.

"You don't have the stake in this that I do," she said. "You're just a scientist who got curious about a problem related to science. But for me, when it comes to Una Vida, it's bigger than science, a lot bigger."

"I am taking you to see her now," Cruz said. "We will work together to do what must be done."

Chapter 12

Cruz felt strangely giddy as he drove slowly from Elysian Fields toward the Garden District. Doing what was not routine, which had occupied more and more of his time lately, had brought a whole new perspective on life that agreed with the blood racing through his veins. Jessica sat beside him, hands folded in her lap. She continued her narration as though rushing to get it off her chest before they arrived.

"She lived with me after Mom died. I gave her my bed and I slept down on a cot in my studio. She went from confusing me with my mother, to my grandmother, the nun from Ursuline, her own mother – who I never knew a thing about before...but I didn't care. I was glad to take care of her. I had a purpose," Jessica said.

"And what happened to change all that?" Cruz asked.

Jessica told him that she'd gone out early in the morning a couple of weeks earlier to renew the license for her pottery booth at the French Market. She'd been up most of the night touching up the pieces that had recently come out of the kiln. By sunrise she had about thirty new pieces to sell on Sunday. She was excited with the developing quality of her work, and since it was the tourist season, she thought she had a good chance to make enough money to pay off some of her debts.

But when she came back with her license renewal she was horrified to find Una Vida's precious sheet music ripped to shreds and spread across the living room. Then she found Una Vida in the studio sniffing her finished vases, cups, and bowls; and smashing them one by one, the way the Midrash tells us Abraham once did in his father's idol maker shop. Only five of her pieces were left unbroken when she walked in. Jessica tried to grab Una Vida and get the artifacts away from her, but in a rage, Una Vida threw Jessica to the floor in an act of almost superhuman strength. Then she just continued to sniff and smash as Jessica lay on the floor among the shards. Una Vida kept raving that the containers were filled with Jamaican Ginger and would ruin her life and kill her father.

She was beside herself and adrift in a world that Jessica didn't know how to enter or control. All Jessica knew was that her labor was in pieces, and her patience with it. Upset, sleep-deprived, and still in the wake of grief over a mother she'd never taken the time to know as an adult, Jessica threw Una Vida out of the house. She told her she couldn't take it anymore.

And at that Una Vida calmed and, as if reciting a script that had grown comfortable over the years, she said, "Yes, Mama, I ain't never gonna look back. I found me my bird now, and he lifted me up on his wings."

"What was she talking about?" Cruz asked.

Jessica shook her head. "I don't know, but she talked about being free as a bird all the time. She had a thing about birds…All that happened over a month ago." Jessica's eyes widened as they slowed at the approach to Cruz's house. "I was an idiot," she said.

"Righteous anger doesn't make you an idiot," Cruz offered.

"She tore up her music because she couldn't read anymore. That's why she broke my stuff."

"She doesn't need to read," Cruz said. "She knows it by heart."

Elvira opened the door for them before Cruz could bring his key to the lock.

"This is Jessica," he said with a smile.

"Welcome to our home, Jessica." Elvira took her hand and gently coaxed her through the door. Then, as if in answer to the unspoken question on Jessica's face, she announced, "Una Vida is asleep."

"She won't recognize me anyway," Jessica said. "Ever since I threw her out, she doesn't know me at all."

"Let's see what happens in the morning," Cruz said. "Tonight, just get a good night's sleep. You're safe here."

"Safe from myself; is that what you mean?" Jessica smiled wearily.

"I've got a bed all made up for you, in Hernan's old room," Elvira said. "I'll show you the way."

*

Jessica answered Cruz's knock on the door of Hernan's old bedroom looking well rested. He invited her down for coffee and when he saw the nervous look she gave him, added, "Elvira took Una Vida down to the levee already. She's been up for hours."

Jessica looked as if she had something important to tell him, something she'd forgotten; but she waited until she'd half-finished her first cup of Community before she spoke.

"It's really weird because I never dream, but I had this

vivid dream last night. I was lost in this field in the middle
of the countryside. I had a message in my hand, this note.
But I couldn't find anyone. I kept getting lost and the corn
kept growing. I looked down at the letter in my hand and
saw a name on the envelope, 'Parker,' is all it said."

"Go on," Cruz prompted. "I know more than a little bit
about cornfield dreams myself," he chuckled.

"That's it. I woke up and started jotting things down
in my journal." She showed him the beaten-up drugstore
notebook she'd carried to the table with her, opened it to a
page filled with scribbles. "It's amazing. I wasn't afraid of the
dream anymore. I kept rewriting the word 'corn,' just got real
obsessed with it, wound up writing the word 'maize' beside
it. And that's when it hit me. My parents knew Una Vida as
Mazy; that was her name."

Jessica spoke as if she'd been told it all by a shaman; she
was completely convinced of its truth. Cruz wasn't sure if
she was manic, experiencing a side effect of having survived
a suicide attempt, or hallucinating. But the fact that she had
dreamed of corn in the house where he'd been haunted by
cornfield dreams for months forced him to acknowledge
that everything was happening the way it was meant to
happen, and it didn't matter how or why. It was hardly the
clinical life Jessica had accused him of living.

"What was her last name?" he prodded.

Jessica looked blank. "I…I don't know," she said. "But
I'm going to find Parker."

Jessica spoke the words in a tone that was more alert and
assured than Cruz had ever heard from her. It was a Louis
Armstrong solo at perfect pitch. And though he could not
understand the logic of how it was put together, when he
heard it there was a staggering beauty in it.

"What makes you think you could find him?" Cruz
asked.

"The dream," she said. "It's all plain as day now. I don't know why I kept missing it."

Jessica followed him out into the street and toward his car.

"Where are you going?" she shouted.

"To check on something," he said. "You stay here; make yourself at home."

"I'm coming with you," Jessica called, pulling against the locked passenger door.

Cruz hesitated, and then undid the lock.

"Where are we going?" she asked as he headed down St. Charles.

"The Cornstalk Inn," he answered.

"What? Why?"

Cruz turned and looked Jessica in the eyes. "I dreamed of a corn maze, too, remember?" he finally choked out. "I was lost in there…I've *been* lost in there."

Jessica and Cruz stood on Royal Street in front of the Inn, prepared to search together in a maze of maize – and the woman called Mazy.

*

The manager recognized Cruz at first, then, taking in the woman with him, wrinkled his brow. "How can I help you?" he finally asked.

"I was here the other night with my wife, remember?" Cruz said. "This is Jessica. We're looking for information about…a long-lost relative. We think she might have stayed here a long time ago."

It was Jessica's turn to look puzzled. Fortunately the manager was looking at Cruz, weighing the benefits of co-operating.

"We don't want to trouble you," Cruz continued. "But

I'm just wondering how far back the guest book you keep in the lobby goes."

Jessica didn't see the neatly palmed fifty dollar bill that made its way from Cruz's hand to the manager's. The open book in front of them was nearly half-filled, but the manager was looking at the shelf below it, covered by a glass door.

"It goes back to the beginning," he said. "One book after another."

"Do you mind if we look? We'll just sit right here, if you'll allow us."

The manager grunted, then shrugged. "As long as you don't interfere with the guests coming and going," he allowed.

Cruz smiled.

It took twenty minutes to find what Cruz was looking for – an entry, in January, 1935, that spelled out a missing piece of the puzzle Cruz had been destined to jigsaw together:

"Charley Parker"

The name was scrawled in bold calligraphy, with a feather deftly drawn between the first name and the last. Charley Bird Parker, though history didn't record it, had spent two nights at the Cornstalk Inn the year before he went back to New York and completed his physical and mental disintegration at Bellevue.

"Omigod." Jessica's exclamation brought Cruz's mind back from reeling at the discovery that Una Vida had been with Charley Bird. Jessica was pointing at something on the next line, an even harder-to-read scrawl, a Freudian slip so uncanny that it was powerful enough to plant Cruz's field of dreams seventy years in the future –

"Mazy"

In the same unmistakable calligraphy, the word was followed by a hasty but nonetheless effective drawing of what could only be the fountain in the Inn's courtyard – the soothing sound of which had induced Cruz's powerful dream.

"I've got it," Cruz said, accepting the thought his brain sent him without hesitation from a place so distant he was sure he'd never discover its location. "Her name was Mazy Waters."

"That's it!" Jessica jumped to her feet. "Now I remember. Her son was named Parker."

Cruz gave the directory a final glance to confirm the other piece of data he'd acquired: "23" was written neatly in faded pencil next to the names. The lovers had stayed in the same room Cruz and Elvira had occupied to incubate the most vivid of his cornfield dreams.

Chapter 13

Cruz's cell phone rang on the way back to his house. It was Malta Park's director, letting him know that the room on St. John's had opened up.

"You can bring her in anytime today," the director said.

Cruz's immediate response surprised even himself. "I appreciate that, but it won't be necessary. I want to keep her at our home for now. I've had a breakthrough and I want to play it out before deciding what to do."

"Shall I hold the room? It was Raymond's father's," he added. "He passed."

"I'm so sorry to hear that. Please give Raymond my sympathies. As for the room, give it to the next person who needs it. I'll have to take my chances." He looked over at Jessica, remembering the broken tea mug. "Not everything broken remains so."

He knew now that he was the glue that would somehow, with the help of the serendipity that dogged his heels and led him on, piece together Una Vida's identity.

*

Una Vida and Elvira walked downstairs and into the kitchen where Cruz had taken Jessica for Argentinean mate. He watched as the two women confronted each other.

"Hello, Una Vida," Jessica said, moving toward her for a hug.

Una Vida seemed to shrink inside herself, looking at Elvira as though for help and refusing to meet Jessica's eyes. "I don't know you," she finally said. "Do I know you?"

"I'm sorry I was mean to you," Jessica said, her tone contrite.

"I don't know what you're talking about. Is she talking to me?" Una Vida looked to Cruz for help.

"It's time to hang the clothes out on the line to dry," Elvira said to Una Vida, taking her elbow and guiding her toward the door to the yard. "You understand – "

"I told Dr. Cruz she wouldn't know me," Jessica interrupted. "It's okay."

"Come into my office." Cruz picked up Jessica's tea cup and carried it, with his own, toward the den, nodding for her to follow him. "Let's do some investigating on the Internet."

To study the brain was to witness history and progress. The Internet was the brain's new colony, perhaps its ultimate exterior colony – the conclave cave that was as unlimited as the universe within. Cruz always approached the Internet with a feeling of respect akin to the sensation of peering into his electron microscope at actual brain tissue. The Internet was the species' brain's self-portrait in full chaotic motion and unending connection. Even the act of Googling was a perfect mirror of brain operation; you entered a random word and the richest of associations appeared before your eyes within microseconds.

A web without a thread of beginning or end, the language of the Internet was *connection*. One fact led to another, things could be constantly compared – searched for references, phrases, even lyrics to songs. We use the Internet with such pleasure, Cruz thought, because we've finally created a tool that can keep up with our questions, our endless thirst for knowledge, and the speed with which we have a tendency to turn any answer into our next question. The Internet is the brain's mirror, its counterpart; there is nothing cold or alien about it. Its technology is not simply the outgrowth of economics or scientific rationale; it's more akin to an art form that responds to a deep down human need. Once upon a time, the oral tradition – in which entire cultures were transmitted only through memory and word of mouth – gave way to the print tradition that came into its own with Gutenberg's printing press. Cruz felt enormously privileged to be living in a time when the print tradition was giving way to the Internet.

For the brain, there is no resolution to life's aching questions; there is only communication, internal dialogue that ceases only when we contemplate the stillness beyond ourselves. The Internet is the same – always a new piece of information, always an open case – but never the stillness. The stillness is left to us. The Internet is a great leap on the developmental scale of putting our thinking into action. More than utilitarian, the Internet isn't a conscious outcome of the thinking brain, but a portrait of the thinking brain itself with all of its messy pop-up boxes, hyperlinks, and key word searches we conjure on a daily basis.

The excitement Cruz felt as his fingers flew over the keyboard – with Jessica looking on without a clue to his brain's commentary on the splendors of cyberspace – was that the Internet freed the brain to do what it did best: not simply gathering data or chronicling opinion, but deciphering and analyzing it. How will the human brain evolve, he wondered, once it gets used to the fact that it doesn't need to remember the things that are now just a few keystrokes away? Will we become better thinkers, be better equipped to hold different opinions on the same issue in the same mind in the same moment? If so, we'll see further than we ever have and be more open than we've ever dreamed. What for so long seemed like an inborn instinctual necessity – the drive to compete – might even give way to a new evolutionary web-model, the sort that produces an instinctual drive to interactively cooperate for the benefit of mutual survival.

But Google awaited him. He typed in "Una Vida." Almost nine million entries greeted him and he remembered the hour he'd spent a few weeks earlier trying to sort it out and finding nothing but frustration. He'd seen references to a jazz singer by that stage name, but always in context with more important folks – Coltrane, Armstrong, Parker, Brubeck. "Mazy Waters" was a little better – only 9,890 entries – so he added "+ jazz" to the search request and got it down to 229 entries on ten pages. Four of them concerned the jazz singer. Jessica seemed to sense what he was doing, though Cruz suspected she'd never actually used a keyboard.

"Where do they send children waiting for adoption?"

Cruz gave her a glance of acknowledgment that he could see pleased her. Within minutes, he was looking at foster homes in Iowa – well over 6,000 entries. He tried "foster homes + Iowa + Louisiana" and was dismayed that he'd have to scan over 200,000 entries to find what he was looking for. Then he looked at the page again.

The twenty-first entry brought gooseflesh to his arms: "Calcasieu Baptist Children's Home...Iowa, Louisiana."

*

When he got out of the shower and looked out his back

184

window, Cruz saw Elvira on a ladder tying up line between two live oaks. Una Vida had a stack of towels in her hands and was throwing them over the line. Elvira couldn't find clothespins to accommodate the fantasy completely, but Una Vida didn't seem to mind. The scene made Cruz think of all the times he'd looked out and seen Elvira playing along with whatever their daughters, Patricia and Andrea, wanted to pretend about. She'd go with the whims of their fantasies all day long on the weekends.

"Don't stifle their imaginations," she'd tell Cruz. "They're learning how to become who they need to be – they're practicing," she would say.

With Una Vida, it was as if life was going in a circle, back to the beginning. He was watching her transform from one character to another, from one moment in time to another.

Cruz went outside, thinking how nice it was to see clothes out on the line – that he hadn't remembered seeing a clothesline in their yard since they lived in Argentina. It seemed silly not to use a clothesline when New Orleans' climate was so tropical.

"Look at how fast these towels are drying," Elvira said by way of greeting.

Una Vida looked pleased with herself. The matching towels on the line made Cruz think of his school uniforms hanging behind his mother's house, all the neatly lined up white button-up shirts and the navy blue pants. He saw his father's work shirts and his mother's aprons blowing in the wind of his childhood, drying and bearing the smell of the mountains of Tucuman. Una Vida's fantasy had brought him back to a reality he hadn't thought of in years. But wasn't that memory another form of fantasy? The beige, white, and blue thick terry cloth towels hanging on the line were the entryway for three minds – maybe four if Jessica was watching from the window – to create meaningful worlds. Cruz's childhood, Elvira's early life as a mother, and Una Vida's life as a helper to Ella – Cruz couldn't help but be struck by how little input from the outside the mind needed to create a world.

Una Vida, reverting to childhood, had picked up the garden hose and was trying to shake water from it, holding it to her mouth. Cruz and Elvira exchanged glances. He quickly explained what he'd found out and told her that he and Jessica would be driving to Iowa, Louisiana – nearly all the way to Lake Charles, on the western side of the state near the Texas border – to see if the trail to the identity of Una Vida's son could be picked up there.

"How do you know that's where he was?"

"It's all falling into place," Cruz said. "Una Vida was afraid he'd live in a cornfield. She associated cornfields with Iowa. There's a foster home in Iowa, Louisiana. I'm sure she didn't know that."

"I'm sure she did." Elvira had a strange look on her face.

"What?" Cruz asked.

"She told me about her two nights with Charlie Parker, though she didn't use his name. Just called him Bird.'"

"She told you?"

"Well, not exactly. She talked about it when we were doing the wash this morning. I'm not sure she knew who she was talking to, but I happened to be the one with her. She told me it was *her* idea that they stay at the Cornstalk Inn; that he bribed the innkeeper, who could care less about the Jim Crow laws if the price was right, to let them use a back room; that he played his saxophone just for her, in the early morning after the first rooster crowed, on their balcony. Because she'd heard about the Cornstalk's history, and said someday *she'd* be going back home to Iowa; she missed it so much."

Elvira also told Cruz she didn't think Jessica should be traveling after what she'd just been through. All the rational parts of Cruz agreed. But those parts weren't in charge of his brain at that moment; if the rational part wanted to tag along on the journey, it would have to do so as a passenger. Elvira's latest information confirmed his decision. By any rational standard, it didn't add up.

Chapter 14

Jessica didn't feel like talking. As Cruz guided the car westward on I-10 across the Bonnet-Carre Spillway Bridge, they listened to Thelonious Monk. The prayer of St. John and a monk who took their vows in the monasteries of 52nd Street carried Cruz and Jessica along toward the key to Una Vida's very identity.

By 1955, Bird had died of heart failure, pneumonia, and cirrhosis of the liver at thirty-four – with the "body of a sixty-four-year-old man," according to the coroner. But he'd invented a new music, bebop, reaching with his instrument to places no one had reached; he was listening to a muse all his own. Despite that mastery, he was unable to control the addiction; he was a heroin addict and any time he tried to quit the drug he became a raging alcoholic.

One of his greatest admirers and protégés, the young Miles Davis, was also a heroin addict by 1954. But that year, Miles asked his father to lock him in his second-floor studio without his trumpet so he could kick his habit cold turkey. Despite burning joints, pounding head, violent shakes, shivers, and frightening hallucinations, Davis held fast and emerged from the room a week later to walk on the freshly mowed grass of his father's acreage and look up at the sun. His father gave him back his trumpet when he saw the look in Miles' eyes.

How did Miles Davis succeed, where Parker failed? Was it a matter of free will? Some people would call such spontaneous healing a miracle. St. Anthony certainly would have. Jessica's grandparents believed that Una Vida's appearance in their lives was nothing short of a miracle.

By 1968, the last club on 52nd Street had closed its doors. The Five Spot, where Willem De Kooning and Jackson Pollack hung out to listen to Coltrane, was gone. By 1974, both Louis Armstrong and Duke Ellington were dead. In 1975, Miles Davis declared jazz dead. He called it "the music of the museum." Where it had once accounted for seventy percent of American record sales, in that year it was only three percent. But it was all alive in Una Vida, and Cruz knew it.

Without knowing what provoked it, Cruz told Jessica about his mother's death. She listened with sympathy as he explained why he hadn't rushed back after receiving Elvira's summons and nodded when he explained his rationalization about focusing on something he *could* change. But her nod was wholehearted when he confessed he'd come to realize that rationalization didn't excuse him. He should have jumped on that plane and made the effort.

"I should have gone to my grandfather's funeral," she said. "If you had gotten back in time, what would you have done?"

Cruz took his eyes off the road to meet hers. "It would've been enough to just hold her hand."

*

They reached Baton Rouge in an hour and a half, a little longer than the usual time it took Cruz to drive to the campus for his annual lecture. i-10 had been bottlenecked due to a three-car pileup. From Baton Rouge, it took them less than an hour to cross Atchafalaya Swamp and reach Lafayette. Forty-five minutes later, Cruz saw the "Iowa" exit in his rearview mirror; he also saw flashing red lights. He looked at the dashboard to see he'd been doing eighty-five.

But instead of a ticket, the highway patrolman who stopped them ended up providing them with a police escort to the front steps of the Calcasieu Baptist Children's Home, a hideous 1960s construction, fortunately hidden in a grove of live oaks dripping with Spanish moss. The patrolman had taken one look at Cruz's name and told him he'd listened to him speak fifteen years ago when he'd thought about studying medicine.

"I chose police work instead," he laughed. "Less stress."

*

The patrolman insisted on escorting them into the building and introducing them to the man in charge. "Otherwise, he won't lift a finger," he said. "He's one of my fishing pals."

Pero Adashek was a tall man whose coke-bottle glasses made his eyes seem as if they were peering out from a tunnel. His stomach looked as if it held at least one bowling ball within; the rest of him was thin as a rail. He spoke out of the side of his mouth and spittle was constantly being drawn to the left corner of his lips. The more he spoke, the more the spittle grew into a white milk-like substance.

After giving Cruz and Jessica a brief history of the last hundred years of the home – it had originally been Catholic, a plantation home, torn down by the state during Huey P. Long's governorship to make way for the present structure that was so ugly that only abstemious Baptists could stand it – finally told them that for the last twenty years, when a child entered the system the department purged their records three years after the child aged out of the system. By the time Parker was twenty-one, he was out of their files.

"What happens to the purged files?" Cruz asked.

"They're kept in the Parish Hall," Adashek answered. "For ten years. Then they're destroyed."

But in the end, Adashek was helpful, no doubt because of his fishing pal's introduction. He told Jessica after Cruz had excused himself to the bathroom that whenever parental rights were voluntarily terminated there would have had to have been a court hearing and that the courts might have a record.

To get access to the court records took waiting all afternoon. At nearly six, when Cruz became resigned to having to spend the night in Lake Charles or wherever he could find a motel for them, the clerk came back with a smile.

"Now let's see what we can do to help you."

"I hate to keep you here late," Cruz said.

"Honey," the woman replied, "*nobody* keeps me anywhere I don't want to be. Y'all have been waiting, and it's the least I can do."

Within minutes Cruz and Jessica understood why the clerk had been so easygoing. She was obviously highly organized and returned with a smile and a small stack of index cards. Riffling through them, Cruz could see the first were in a neat handwriting and the last few looked like they'd been generated by a word processor.

"Yes, Mazy Waters signed the boy in."

Jessica and Cruz exchanged glances. They were thinking of the Corn Maiden and the cathedral garden and monsters turned allies and destiny and why Amité Deerkill knew so much about it. It was quite a thing to not understand they were doing what they were doing yet feel completely compelled to do it, as if the whole world depended on it. And that was how it was for the both of them, messengers sent to accomplish something that was bigger than themselves.

"She said 'they took my child away,'" Cruz told the clerk.

"They often remember it that way. Women don't like to admit they brought their own children in to become wards of the state." She looked back down at the cards. "The boy – his name was Parker – was sent to St. Anthony's Home for Boys."

Cruz and Jessica reacted as one. They had met under the statue of St. Anthony.

"Now I remember," Jessica said. "That's right. I remember my mother told me Una Vida claimed that St. Anthony was watching over her baby."

"That's why we met in the garden?"

Jessica had no answer. She turned to the clerk.

"I'm confused – "

The clerk read her mind. "I'm sorry. I thought y'all knew that. St. Anthony's was what they called it before the Baptists took it over. Now it's Calcasieu Parish." The wind rattled the windows, shaking the building to let them know a prairie thunderstorm was about to strike. "We'd better close up," the clerk said, "unless y'all brought umbrellas." Efficiently she escorted them out the door, and then followed them, locking it behind her.

"Grover Rees might help you," she added. To Cruz's puzzled expression, she immediately explained, "He was the administrator of the Catholic home. Retired when the Baptists took over. He lives on near the old bridge, in Breaux Bridge. Can't miss it. Biggest house in town, right on Bayou Teche."

Cruz thanked her.

"I'll call ahead; tell him y'all will stop by for coffee in the morning."

As they walked to the car under a dramatically darkened sky, Cruz and Jessica were both giddy from all of it – the events of the day, the sense of adventure, the smell of the approaching rain. The rain came down in buckets. The force of its momentum carried them and, though they didn't know quite where they were headed at the moment, they didn't feel lost. When the downpour finally got to be too much – visibility was near zero, the drops on the windshield as big as pies – Cruz pulled into the only shelter he could find that looked sturdy, wooden, and warm.

The decor at Gauchaux's was bare sidewalls, the fare country, and without hesitation Cruz ordered a dozen crawfish boudin balls. The jovial man behind the counter dropped them into his fryer and pointed to a cooler, where they helped themselves to cold beer. The boudin, tender enough to be cut with the side of their forks and crispy enough to be addictive, melted in their mouths. They ate in silence beneath the fogged-up windows while the downpour continued announcing its determination on the tin roof of the restaurant.

Even more suddenly than it had begun, the rain ceased.

Cruz drove carefully in and out of showers and sunset rainbows as they headed through the rice fields east toward Breaux Bridge. Just over an hour later they were checked into the Bayou Teche, one of the most charming bed and breakfasts Cruz had seen in Louisiana. He suddenly wished he'd persuaded Elvira to come along. The restored vintage Acadian boarding house proclaimed it was the oldest historical structure in town – and it was directly across from Rees' mansion, which dominated a green lawn leading down to the bayou on the other side.

Cruz completed the check-in process, ignoring the proprietor's glances, and bid Jessica goodnight at the door of
her room. "We'll get an early start?" he dictated, more than
asked. "Country people are morning people, and I'd still like
to be back at work by one." Jessica nodded.

In his slightly over-comfortable room, Cruz was pleasantly surprised to find a wireless connection. The Internet's
reach apparently extended even to the heart of bayou country. He went online to read the day's papers and responses
of the neuroscience conference, then spent an hour on the
phone with Elvira going over every detail. He wanted to
make sure she'd gotten the contact information of the Alzheimer presenters. Then he told her what he'd discovered
about Mazy checking her own child into the orphanage.
And about the bed and breakfast.

"We will definitely have to come back for a weekend,"
he added.

*

Over coffee on the white-frame porch the next morning,
Cruz learned that he wasn't the only one who hadn't slept
well. Jessica, too, kept waiting for dreams that didn't come
and tossed and turned, checking her bedside clock.

"Maybe we're at that point where dreams end and reality begins," Cruz said.

Jessica looked at him. "Not bad for a scientist," she said.
"I kept waiting to dream of cornfields, but nothing came."

Gazing across the pleasantly serene bayou, Cruz understood immediately why the home of Grover Rees, framed
with willows and Spanish moss-draped oaks, had graced the
cover of a national magazine. All it needed was the stars and
bars to be the epitome of everything Southern. They continued with their coffee until they saw the blinds rising in

the windows of the brick mansion. Then they drove across the old bridge that gave the town its name.

When they arrived at the door and rang the bell, a voice came over the intercom to ask them to identify themselves. They did so and Cruz could hear the door latch open.

"Come on in," the same voice invited them. "I've been expecting you."

Rees rolled out of his office in a wheelchair and led them back into the small room overtaken by filing cabinets and shelves of loose-leaf binders.

"When I left the home," he explained, "I guess I brought all my work with me. Now with my wife gone, it's all I have left." He didn't sound like a man who felt sorry for himself.

The small talk was brief. To Cruz's comments about the house, Rees explained that his wife, Constance Breaux, was descended from the founding family of the town. She'd inherited the home that once stood on that very spot; they'd built around it to create the present domicile.

Cruz showed him the court file for Parker Waters. Jessica asked the former director if Parker Waters might have been adopted from St. Anthony's Home. The clerk at the courthouse had told them that if Parker *had* been adopted, they might be out of luck because his name would have been changed. Rees told them that he didn't remember the boy, but that his memory wasn't what it once had been – and that an adoption of a five-year-old African-American kid from St. Anthony's was highly unlikely in those years. If Parker had been there, he added, there'd be a record of him in one of his files. He gestured to the collection of file cabinets.

"I'm afraid I'm not digitized yet – probably never will be – but I have all this data here, all these paper files sitting here, and most of the time they do the job."

Cruz reflected on the discrepancy between Rees' filing system and the Internet.

As though reading his mind, Rees said, "Yes, I'm living in the stone age. That's where I've lived all my life and that's where I'll remain."

He rolled toward the corner, where Cruz saw an entryway he hadn't noticed before. Gesturing for them to follow, Rees led them to an office half the size of the one they'd been in with files crammed so high to the ceiling it looked like a precarious skyline that might fall at any moment – or like the walls of yet another labyrinth, Cruz thought. But the old director knew how to navigate that city of the dead and did so with an agility and purposefulness that left Cruz and Jessica impressed and grateful.

A woman, who looked even older than Rees, entered with an ornate silver tray, upon which was impeccably presented an old-fashioned coffee service. She offered half-full cups to Jessica and Cruz, who took them obediently, though they'd had more than their fill at the bed & breakfast. But the service was so elegant that neither of them could have imagined saying no.

After a few falling boxes and a rather intense search on the part of a determined Rees, they learned that Parker Waters had been a resident at St. Anthony's until he was seventeen. But unlike a Google search, the trail didn't continue – only a yellowed typewriter page with the barest of details. Cruz glanced at Jessica and saw a similar deflating in her as the anticlimactic end to their quest sank in.

Even Rees appeared to sense their disappointment when Cruz looked up from the discharge letter and said, "That's it, then. Thanks for your help."

The old woman returned to inform Rees that he had a telephone call and he excused himself, leaving them alone in the warehouse of memory their host had fashioned in an era before the Internet. Cruz marveled at the man's ability to pull a needle out of the haystack of files and cabinets that he and time had created. But facts were often bloodless, and Parker Waters seemed as distant a figure as ever.

"What now?" Jessica asked.

"Nothing more to do here...go home, I suppose."

Cruz wondered if the absence of dreams the previous night had somehow been a signal from his unconscious mind that they were off-track. Or perhaps destiny had no hand on the tiller, after all. Had the random confluence of events and their subconscious minds simply failed, at last, to form a discernible pattern? No. Even his empirical mind told Cruz there was too much in play for it all to be an unlikely run of coincidence finally spent.

Jessica was gathering herself to leave when she saw the gleam in his eyes.

"Wait," Cruz said, with authority that surprised even himself. "There's more to learn here than records can tell us. I can feel it."

Jessica smiled, a radiant expression of hope renewed. "Me, too."

As if on cue, Rees wheeled back into the room. "Anything else I can do for y'all?"

"Yes," Cruz said, following his intuition with each word, "Do you know of anyone left from Parker's era here? Someone who might remember him?"

Rees pondered the question before responding. "He doesn't answer his phone much anymore, but Buddy Aguillard is still alive and kicking. He worked at St. Anthony's for almost fifty years. He was a favorite of the boys and kept in touch with most of them. He was a bachelor all his life and acted like a father to those boys – the place was always losing money then, but it was Buddy's place. He lived in this house as house manager for almost his whole adult life. Most kids come out of college and work with 'troubled kids' because they can't find other work and need a place to live rent-free.

Most of the workers nowadays are as troubled as the kids are – here to solve their own problems. But Buddy helped everybody, he's a legend around here," the director said.

Cruz and Jessica exchanged glances. So there was more to find there, after all.

Rees led them to the living room, its ceiling-to-floor French windows framed with gardenias and giant pink hibiscus, which faced across the bayou at the porch where Cruz and Jessica had begun the morning.

"No answer," Rees said, cradling his antique rotary phone. "But that old dinosaur lives just down the road."

*

It was only a five-minute walk to the white-framed railroad house Rees had described. An aged and scrawny hound chained in the overgrown yard gave them a rather ornery look as Cruz and Jessica approached.

"Easy, boy," Cruz said, warily edging up the walk.

Weeds split its old stones and had turned them at odd angles. Then he froze at an explosion of barks as the chain clinked and the dog took a step toward him.

"Be careful, Dr. Cruz," Jessica said from the safety of the road. "His chain will reach – "

Cruz glanced to his side and saw that he could beat a hasty retreat if necessary. He took another step toward the front door, determined. A curtain stirred at the window. The dog eyed Cruz suspiciously, lip curling over yellowed teeth. But the door opened.

"Chauncey! Sit, boy," said an eminently good-natured voice.

Its owner ducked his head to step onto the porch – Buddy Aguillard was well over six feet tall. He had the long thin bones of a basketball player and droopy molasses-colored skin. Much of both were uncovered by a v-neck tee and gym shorts. The dog mellowed and squatted obediently on its haunches, tail wagging.

"Old Chauncey fancies himself a guard dog," Buddy said. "Keeps the kids from egging my house, I guess."

Ten minutes later, they were inside Buddy's musty but well-ordered home, standing before an impressive wall of framed black-and-white photographs. They were all the same – rows of grinning boys in caps and gowns – but spanning generations.

"This is my Wall of Fame," Buddy said.

He scanned the array of pictures, finally pulling down one that even Cruz couldn't have reached without a step-stool.

"Here he is," Buddy said, pointing out a sweet-faced kid as he handed the slightly dusty frame to Cruz.

"You remember Parker?" Jessica asked.

"How could I forget him?"

Buddy poured himself a coffee from a tray that sat on the table in front of them and then opened the plastic on a pack of graham crackers and carefully broke them on the dotted line before setting them on a large green plate.

After rummaging around awhile, Buddy showed them photos of Parker at age eighteen, twenty-two, twenty-six, and thirty-one. He told them, stumbling over the word, that Parker had earned a Ph.D. in a field called Ethnomusicology. That his specialty was jazz. That he knew more about jazz than anyone had a right to know.

"Parker always had an ear for music. Always wanted to play – and, boy, could he! Used all the money he made working after school to buy records and to sneak into bars to hear jazz. He told us back then that his mama was a jazz singer and that she'd be coming back for him. He'd look for her name in the trades or on the marquee and in the record stores, but he never found it."

What Buddy told them next made Cruz's gooseflesh reappear.

"I used to work the boys in the cornfield, so we could help feed ourselves – store-bought food was expensive back then – "

"Cornfield?" Jessica interrupted, her eyes widening with surprise.

Buddy nodded. "The whole countryside was corn in those days. Rotated it with cotton. That's why they named the town Iowa. Now it's all rice and beans, but we used to grow the sweetest white corn you ever ate. Made it into *maque chou*, with lots of pepper and a little tomato and onion."

Cruz nodded his appreciation of this Cajun side dish, which he'd tasted more than once at Domelises's in New Orleans.

"Parker weren't much good working the field," Buddy went on. "But he was sure something with the banjo."

Cruz was stunned. The dream and reality had come together. Synchronicity – dreams, St. Anthony, the Cornstalk Inn, tarot cards – had all worked their purposes on him and had led him inevitably to that moment. His only credit was having the good sense to listen to the words of his mother in the dreams.

"He'd bring it along with him and we'd let him play the blues in the field. Kept the other boys in good spirits while they worked. They was more productive than when Parker was trying to cut the corn hisself. Eventually Parker let go of all that talk about his mother like most boys do and just got to the business of growing up and getting on with his life." Buddy soaked the bites of graham cracker in the coffee to soften it as he slipped it into a mouth mostly emptied of teeth. "I used to tell those boys...ain't nothing you can do about what been done to you, all can be done is make the most of your life from this point on. Sometimes a man gotta learn how to raise himself. I did it that way, and it was my mission to teach that to those boys. Parker was slow to catch onto that at first. He kept hold of that fantasy of his mama for a long time. But one day he just buried it. I remember that day because it was the day he told me he was going to go to college to become his own man. And he did, too; used that music to get himself a scholarship to Tulane," Buddy said proudly.

Buddy's collection included photographs of a grown-up Parker playing in an orchestra; he even showed them the Christmas cards Parker sent every year. Buddy had his box of letters, just like Jessica and Cruz and Rees did, except his was a solid wall of lives and pictures and hopes and regrets and confessions. Buddy's "Wall of Fame" was yet another form of memory, a genealogy of happenstance that kept those orphaned boys clasped together under the wings of St. Anthony and held there by a man whose heart was bigger than any one body could comfortably contain. Buddy's size made Cruz think of Corey's monster, providing all that extra life to those that needed it.

Cruz and Jessica stayed awhile with Buddy Aguillard poring over boxes and catching up on Parker and his love affair with music in all parts of the world. Buddy was a proud father.

"When was the last time you heard from him?"

Buddy reverently removed another photo from an overstuffed album. "This is the last one he sent me," he said.

Cruz took it from him, a color photo of Parker as a middle-aged man in a suit. From the style of the suit and the length of his hair, Cruz placed the photo somewhere in the 1980s. Buddy told them, almost apologetically, that Parker hadn't been in touch over the last few years – like many of the boys, once the "looking back started to get in the way of looking forward."

Cruz stared at the photograph a long while then for whatever reason, he reached and turned it over and saw the faded words.

Jessica read them aloud: "Dr. Parker Waters, Associate Professor Ethnomusicology, University of New Orleans, 1983."

Cruz stared at the words for several moments to make sure what he was seeing was real.

"It's funny," he finally said, "that the things you work the hardest to find turn out to be right under your nose."

It reminded Cruz of a Hassidic tale Morton Friedman had told him once about a man named Elek. Elek was from Krakow, Poland. He had a dream that a treasure was buried under a bridge in Prague, Czechoslovakia. He made the long journey there and met a guard at the bridge who he feared would question his digging, so he told him his dream and offered to share half the treasure with him if he let him dig. The guard laughed at Elek and refused. He told him that he, too, had had a dream, a dream of a treasure buried under the stove of a poor Jew in Krakow.

"Imagine if I'd been silly enough to follow that dream," the guard laughed again. "Now get out of here."

Elek picked up his shovel and ran all the way back to Krakow. He dug underneath his stove, and sure enough the treasure was there.

Cruz thought how his meeting on a levee led to a meeting in St. Anthony's garden and that morning's meeting with the former director of the orphanage once known as St. Anthony's – and he'd just learned that the man they were seeking had been in New Orleans all along.

Cruz and Jessica walked silently back to the car. On the drive back to New Orleans, they went over what they'd learned and worked together to piece together as many pieces as they could of the puzzle that was Una Vida. Jessica was more focused than he'd seen her – ever since he told her the story of his mother.

They got off the freeway and pulled into a gas station that boasted both a casino and an Internet café. Cruz got onto the Internet, Googled "Dr. Parker Waters," and there it was: Professor of Ethnomusicology, with a specialty in African music. He had been teaching at the University of New Orleans for the last twenty-five years. All Cruz could think of was Elek and the treasure right under his own stove. He told the story to Jessica. She burst into laughter that became tears and Cruz laughed, too. How could he have not thought to Google that name before? With all its genius, the brain could get so focused on one detail that it could miss something obvious. Of course, how would he have known that the boy would have retained his mother's last name or be accomplished enough to be an Internet presence?

They laughed so hard that a woman sleeping on a bench to get out of the cold woke up and began to laugh with them. Parker Waters worked less than ten miles from Cruz' Institute. The maze had revealed itself, the neurons were firing in unison – whatever you wanted to call it, it was happening and he and Jessica were feeling its pulse.

Back on the road, Cruz called the music department at the University of New Orleans and found out that Dr. Waters had retired two years earlier. He was now a "professor emeritus; just comes to board meetings and graduations," the secretary explained. But she wouldn't give out his personal information without contacting him first. Dr. Waters had requested that his number not be given out.

Chapter 15

Cruz didn't realize why the room looked so familiar at first glance. He went into the bathroom and after washing his face to wake himself up, he opened the mirrored medicine cabinet in front of him. He hadn't planned to be at Malta Park that morning. But it was clear from Elvira's account of her last forty-eight hours with Una Vida that she needed to be in a place where she could have round-the-clock care. His phone call to the director produced the news that room 316 was still available, and Cruz wanted to check it out himself before phoning Elvira to bring Una Vida in.

"Somehow, when you left," Elvira had told him, "it was as though her world fell apart. I think she recognized Jessica and was just being stubborn about admitting it. Then with you both gone, she felt lost. It was almost as if you'd been her anchor all her life." Elvira admitted that she'd given her some red wine to help her calm down.

Cruz stared into the cabinet, not knowing what he expected to find. The motion was habitual. It was the room in which he'd realized Elvira was right about brains being meaningless without humans, the room from which he'd walked away with an *opening* mind. And there, in the cabinet he'd opened for no reason, was the tea cup he'd clumsily broken that morning. Someone had glued it back together perfectly, except for a tiny chip that was too small to attach.

Why had the cup been left there and why had the cleaning crew missed it? It had to have been Raymond who glued it back together. Why had he bothered, when he said he could have just gone home and made another? Cruz took hold of the abandoned cup and closed the empty cabinet. He held onto the cup with both hands, conscious of not wanting to drop something that had already been broken.

"Dr. Cruz? Is that you?" said a voice from the doorway.

Cruz turned to face Raymond. "Just wanted to double check if I left anything." The two men looked into each other's eyes.

"I'm sorry," Cruz finally said, feeling his own awkwardness.

He offered Raymond the cup. Raymond accepted it from his hands, almost reverently.

"Thank you. Of course, it's a blessing. I know that. But he was still my father, and he died."

Cruz nodded and then moved toward the man who suddenly looked so much more like a boy. He wrapped his arms around him in a bear hug and could feel Raymond's spirit accepting the embrace as he slumped momentarily in Cruz's strong arms.

"I guess I needed that," Raymond said. He pulled back. "Thank you. How'd you get in here to do that?" Raymond asked as he looked down at the cup, inspecting it.

"I just found it in the medicine cabinet. I figured you forgot it."

"I never glued that back. I never took it out of the garbage can that day," Raymond said. "You didn't do it yourself?"

Cruz shook his head. Raymond took the cup to the sink, ran water into it, and drank it.

"It still holds water," he said, surprised. "Whoever glued this took their time to line things up just right."

Raymond paused then, thinking of something that took him far from that room of death and passing.

"What?" Cruz asked after a moment.

"Dad used to love putting together these intricate model airplanes. The more pieces, the better. He drove me crazy with them as a kid. For a while he built models in here while he was able, one of the few things he could remember how to do. But in these last days and weeks, there's no way he could have done something like that. Where would he have gotten the glue? One of the maintenance men must have done it when they were bored one night and put it back in that cabinet. Dad never really used that medicine cabinet much. He kept all his stuff in the closet and it was marked just so for him."

Raymond had the logic figured perfectly and was resting in it briefly – when Cruz shook his head.

"Don't think that way," he said. "Accept it." He reached for Raymond's hand and held it. "Rejoice in the knowledge that not everything that's broken remains so and that the glue that holds the parts together is mixed with life and love. That's what your father was telling you by leaving this cup behind."

Raymond smiled, and held the cup up as if in blessing. Then he turned and walked away.

An hour later, prompted by Cruz's phone call, Elvira brought Una Vida to Malta Park. The director talked her into lying down for a nap and Elvira went into the office to fill out forms that took responsibility for Una Vida's care.

*

The next morning, the Dean of Arts and Sciences walked Jessica and Cruz over to the music building. The head of the music department had made a call on Cruz's behalf and the Dean, recognizing the name, was more than happy to help. He presided over their request for Parker's address and phone number and made sure they received them.

Cruz thought of calling ahead, but neither he nor Jessica could figure out what they would say over the phone. Parker's house was a 1910 yellow Victorian with a large wraparound porch and a huge live oak whose roots were pulling up the sidewalk in front of the house. But the feature that struck Cruz was the green wrought iron fence that bordered the front lawn from the sidewalk. Brightly painted, well-maintained, and obviously custom-built, it was identical to the bright green fence surrounding the Corn Stalk Inn on Royal Street.

Undeniably they were in the right place. They heard music, but nobody came to the door to answer Cruz's knock. The bell seemed to be broken.

They walked around to the back, past badly tended clumps of white and blue hydrangeas. Jessica spotted a man at his desk writing. At Cruz's nod, she knocked loudly on the back door until he answered.

A much older, fleshed-out version of his photograph, Parker Waters opened the back door. The office Cruz glimpsed behind him reminded him of his own: stacks covering the floor and nearly every surface in the room. Except those stacks weren't papers and files. They were records and CDs. Parker's shelves were a vertical labyrinth filled with video and audio tapes and reels. He owned a

208

large tape player, a reel-to-reel machine, and all the modern equipment you'd expect to see in any recording studio. On his walls were pictures of musicians in color and black-and-white from what looked like all over the world. Cruz immediately recognized Charlie Parker and Dizzy Gillespie. The room was an entire idiosyncratic world, shaped in the image of Parker.

"If I don't answer the front door, it's because I'm working," Parker said, slamming the door in their faces.

Jessica knocked again loudly. He reopened the door, looked them up and down.

"If you're selling something or running for office, just leave your flyer in the mail slot like everybody else."

His anger at being interrupted turned his face to a caricature – like one of Goya's Black Paintings, Cruz thought. But Jessica had wedged her foot in the door and stopped it from slamming.

She screamed above the music, "My grandmother knew your mother before you were born. Buddy Aguillard sent us here."

Like a man resigned to his fate, Parker opened the door to let Jessica in. Cruz followed.

Parker turned the music off and sat down behind his desk. The silence underlined the strangeness of the moment. He didn't say anything for a long moment, and neither did Cruz or Jessica.

"Buddy sent you?" Parker finally asked.

"He helped us figure out where you were," Jessica answered.

"I haven't exactly been keeping my whereabouts a secret."

"Your mother is Mazy Waters. She became known as Una Vida."

For a split second, Cruz thought he detected something

in Parker's face, but the man's iron mask held and revealed nothing more.

"She lived with my mother, she delivered my mother," Jessica pleaded.

"My mother, whoever she was, gave me away when I was five years old. Buddy raised me, not her. My mother is dead. You shouldn't have come, whoever you are. You had no right to," Parker said.

He stood, regained his composure, and showed them the door again. Cruz, maintaining his dignity, took Jessica by the arm and led her out. He wasn't surprised by the man's first reaction. Parker was shutting the door behind them, but that didn't stop Jessica; she continued to talk right through the door.

"She didn't give you away," Jessica said.

"And your mother is very much alive," Cruz added.

Jessica pulled out the letter from January 1940, which she'd taken with her for the trip to Iowa. She handed it to Parker, who was standing in the half-open door, losing control of his stoic mask.

"My grandmother couldn't answer that call in 1940, but that letter has stayed in my family all these years. Your mother was ordered by the court to take you to an orphanage or they would take you away from her. Yes, she drove you there herself – to the home she chose for you because she was born near Iowa and knew the people would be good people there. This man," she nodded at Cruz, "gave me the courage to put the pieces together, and we're here to bring you to your mother." Jessica voice was clear and strong. "Your mother needs you."

Though Parker stared at the letter, Cruz couldn't be sure he had read the words. He folded it up, placed it carefully back in the envelope, and handed it back to Jessica.

"Maybe twenty years ago…" Parker said with difficulty.

"Even ten. But it's been too long. Too late for her to come back, even if she did it herself. As for this…You might as well be selling steak knives. I'm just not interested."

He gently nudged Jessica off the little back porch, with Cruz following behind. He quietly closed the door behind them.

Making their way to the front of the house, Jessica and Cruz heard the music go back on, louder now than before.

"In five minutes, I'm knocking again," Cruz said.

"Maybe we shouldn't," Jessica frowned. "Maybe it's just too upsetting after all this time. They say some things should be left as they are."

"But all those dreams we both had – "

All of a sudden, the pounding music changed and gave way to Coltrane's "Giant Steps." They listened to it from the front yard for a few minutes and then the door opened.

"You're not going away, are you?" Parker's voice was more a statement than a question.

"She has Alzheimer's," Cruz said. "I doubt she'll know who you are."

"Isn't that just like her, to stay alive and go away at the same time!" Parker's anger flashed. "So then why the hell did you come?"

"Because you'll know her – because we had no choice," Cruz said. "Because I myself am carrying a regret that I wouldn't want anyone else to have to live with."

When Parker didn't move from the porch, Cruz pushed on.

"Your mother's staying at one of the best assisted living facilities in New Orleans – she's at Malta Park, off Magazine Street. We moved her there ourselves."

Parker's hard expression finally softened to sadness.

"Does she remember her music?" he asked tentatively.

"That's the beautiful part. Sometimes she does," Cruz

said. "It's the only thing that brings her alive. But when it does…it's something to see."

Parker took the statement in. "All that music on those buses when I was a kid – I've spent my life traveling the world collecting music in the most obscure places you could imagine. In places where people didn't have electricity and had never even heard or seen a record. All that, all those shelves in there, and I never recorded my own mother's voice. I used to try to remember it. To remember the Bessie Smith tune she used to sing to me. I moved heaven and earth to find her, but got nowhere. After a while you forget. You bury those things," Parker said. "I truly believed she was dead."

"She's still out there," Cruz said. "Still doing Bessie Smith."

"She stopped singing for me a long time ago," Parker said, with finality, and closed the door.

*

Elvira and Cruz went hand-in-hand to Malta Park the next morning. She had listened to her husband's account and told him he'd done everything he could. She was proud of him. It was time to move on.

"It just feels incomplete," Cruz said.

He'd awakened anxious, as if it were the morning of a major presentation at an international conference.

"Maybe, but you've played your part," Elvira said. "If the song is to continue, it's up to the other musicians to pick up the beat."

Cruz nodded, a little wistfully. As he did in his childhood in Argentina when his mother smiled at him, he felt at peace for the first time in months.

Looking fresh and transformed with energy, Jessica was there when they arrived. Una Vida was sitting up eating her breakfast cereal and seemed calm, even smiling at Jessica. When she finished eating, she looked at them with recognition and motioned for her clarinet. Elvira passed her the case while Jessica cleared the tray from the room and Cruz sat down to wait.

Una Vida was fiddling with her reed, not ready to play yet, when Parker Waters walked in.

Cruz stared at him in amazement.

"Is this my mother?" Parker asked.

"Yes," Cruz said. "This is your mother."

"Una Vida," Elvira added.

The three of them stood for a moment, like shy children meeting for the first time at the bus stop on the first day of school. Self-consciously, Cruz and Elvira realized they were holding hands, and let go – though not before Cruz gave hers a squeeze. Her smile showed him it was all the thanks she needed.

Parker approached Una Vida the way he must have approached so many musicians he'd traveled the world over to record. He stood over her awhile, taking her in, accepting the lack of focus in her eyes as she looked back at him. Then she handed him her clarinet, as if passing it on, without knowing why or to whom.

"Can you play that thing?" she asked Parker.

Without a word, Parker took the clarinet.

"Make sure you use a new reed," she said.

Parker put in the new reed Cruz handed him from the box he'd bought her at the store uptown. Parker put his lips to the instrument and played the first tune that came to mind.

Una Vida, to everyone in the room's amazement and disbelief, started to sing the lyrics.

It's a long old road

But I'm gonna find the end…
And when I get there
I'm gonna shake hands with a friend…

Jessica and Elvira moved close to Cruz, leaning into him as silent tears dripped down their faces. Cruz's face was already wet.

Una Vida sang and Parker played the Bessie Smith song with piercing eloquence, not the slightest bit of sentimentality or exaggeration. Una Vida then stopped singing and began to hum the tune with her eyes closed as Parker continued playing. Gradually a smile crossed her face and held. She had found a place inside where she could be happy.

Parker finally let the notes trail off, put the clarinet aside, and simply accompanied his mother's humming with his own much deeper melodic voice. Una Vida took Parker's hand, then reached out for Jessica's with her other hand. She put their hands together.

"Take care of my baby," she said to Jessica. "Thank God y'all brought him back to me."

She turned to look Cruz straight in the eye and gave him such a powerful stare that it took him a moment to realize it was vacant – a stare that reflected an inner world, not the world outside.

"And thank you, Bird, for giving me my baby once and giving him back to me again."

Cruz caught his breath.

As mother and son, Mazy and Parker Waters recognized each other and elevated the moment with music, Cruz, fully present in that unique moment, knew he was witnessing a miracle.

Jessica began to hum the tune as well, and Elvira joined in. Finally Cruz, taking his wife's hand again, added his deep and steady voice; not because he willed it, but because the singing rose from his heart and he couldn't stop it.

The room was filled with the sound of their music. It was one human mind, one life, *una vida*, sharing its deepest resonance.

As the harmony of their voices shaped the molecules in the air around them, Cruz felt himself finally standing in that synaptic meeting ground of reality and dream – the one place in the universe where everything was possible, where power and transcendence were unlimited. Where the crack in his heart was healed. Where man met God.

$\mathscr{A}cknowledgements$

$\mathcal{M}$y heartfelt gratitude goes out to the city New Orleans. The day I arrived in 1981, I was so warmly welcomed that I immediately felt immersed in its culture, its music, and its way of life. Louisiana was very much like the place where I was born and raised – Tucuman, Argentina. Hot, humid, lush with sugarcane and filled with friendly and gracious people – all of these were reminiscent of my homeland, as was the often-contradictory decisions in its pursuits for advancement, yet it felt like home.

My gratitude also extends to the contemporary neuroscience research that aims to understand brain function and to conquer diseases such as Alzheimer's, macular degeneration, retinitis pigmentosa, Parkinson's, epilepsy, depression, schizophrenia, etc. I am grateful because, working as a neuroscientist, I was able to include in this novel reflections on the impact of Alzheimer's disease in daily life.

I am grateful to Jonathon Flaum for helping me in the early stages of this novel. Jonathon's talent provided me with much insight that greatly enriched the story of Una